Also by Jordan Sonnenblick

Drums, Girls & Dangerous Pie

Notes from the Midnight Driver

Zen and the Art of Faking It

After Ever After

Curveball: The Year I Lost My Grip

Falling Over Sideways

THE SECRET SHERIFF OF SIXTH GRADE

Jordan Sonnenblick

Scholastic Inc.

Copyright © 2017 by Jordan Sonnenblick

This book was originally published in hardcover by Scholastic Press in 2017.

ISBN 978-0-545-86321-6

10 9 8 7 6 5 4   21 22 23

Printed in the U.S.A.   40
This edition first printing 2019

Book design by Nina Goffi

To the memory of John "Jack" Kunkle
April 18, 1996–September 18, 2014

Jack, you had the biggest heart in the smallest body, the kindest
soul in the cruelest of situations, and the funniest sense of
humor through the saddest of times. Above all, you were brave,
to a degree I had never seen before I spent time with you.
Thank you for showing me what a hero looks like.

Why I Am the World's Lamest Hero

Let me get a few things out of the way, right from the start.

I can't fly. I'm not even a particularly good jumper. Truthfully, I twisted my ankle so badly during the three-legged race at my third-grade field day that I ended up in the emergency room, along with my partner, Jamie Thompson. Well, most of her. Her two front teeth stayed behind, buried somewhere in the field.

I must be the only superhero in history who's allergic to his sidekick. That would be my trusty hamster companion, Freddy. I have to wash my hands after I hold him, or I break out in hives. In fact, Freddy makes me sneeze so much that I can't even sleep in the same room with him. It's pathetic.

I am incredibly short, but not short enough for the shortness to qualify as a superpower. Like, I am small enough to get stuffed into a gym locker, but not small enough to slip back out through the little air slits. Trust me on this one.

I don't have a fancy costume. I wouldn't look good in one of those clingy leotard things, because to be honest, the leotard wouldn't have anything to cling *to*. I'd be the only hero whose skintight uniform was baggy. It would look like I was melting. Plus, costumes cost money, and having money is another thing that's not one of my superpowers.

Actually, it is totally possible that I have the secret ability to repel money, because for some reason, no cash ever seems to penetrate my anti-dollar force field.

And don't get me started on my weaknesses. The good news is that, as far as I know, I am probably immune to Kryptonite. But that doesn't mean I should challenge Superman to a battle.

Why?

Because I have the worst weakness of all:

I'm weak.

Before

The night before sixth grade, I came home from riding my bike and knew things were bad before I even got close. This was not because I had super-hearing, or ultra vision, or any kind of spooky sixth sense. Everyone could hear the shouting and the crying and the breaking glass. I mean, you couldn't *not* hear it.

My mom was having it out with her latest loser boyfriend, Johnny Something.

I gulped, sped up, and padlocked my bike to the patio of our crummy apartment as fast as I could. Then I opened the back door and stepped into the living room, which looked like a hurricane had just passed through. Mom was sitting on the couch, looking down into her lap, clutching at her left eye, and sobbing. Johnny was leaning over her, shouting so loudly that I could see the spit flying out of his mouth into her hair. There was a bottle on the coffee table. It was three-quarters empty—of course.

Johnny's words were so awful that I started forgetting them even as they went into my ears. Anyway, I had seen this movie a bunch of times before in the years since I had lost my father. There had been a Glenn, a Dave, a Mike, and three Johnnies. My mom *really* liked mean guys named Johnny.

For what felt like minutes, I tried to do something, or say something, or even make a noise. My heart pounded, every hair on my neck stood up, I could feel my face flush—but I couldn't find the guts to move.

Then my mom said, "Shut up, Johnny. Just *shut up*!"

Johnny pulled his right hand way, way back, like a ping-pong player getting ready to hit a slow-moving ball.

He was only a couple of feet away from me. I had time, and he hadn't seen me. I could have picked up a chair and hit him with it. I could have yelled. I could have cleared my throat or whistled.

I could have done *something*.

His hand whipped through the air and cracked across my mother's face so hard her head smashed against the couch

4

cushion and bounced forward again. She barely avoided crashing her face into the table. On the rebound, she looked past Johnny and saw me. He whirled, and his eyes locked on mine.

He smirked and asked, "What are you looking at?" Then he stormed out of the room. A moment later, I heard another sound I recognized from all the other nights like this one: He was throwing his belongings into a suitcase.

My mom wouldn't even look at me again until he was gone, which was all right, because I couldn't face her, either. I couldn't move. I couldn't do anything.

Johnny had said, "What are you looking at?" But that wasn't what he had meant. He had really been saying, "What are you going to do about it?"

The answer was the same as it had been every other time, with two other Johnnies, a Glenn, a Dave, and a Mike:

Nothing.

The First Lesson of Middle School

After Johnny left, I wrapped up some ice in a dish towel for my mother's face—her nose and left eye were already pretty badly swollen—and helped her wash up. Then she staggered off to bed with the homemade ice pack. I listened from the hallway until she started to snore, then went back to check out the situation in the living room.

Other than the glass shards, cigarette butts, and ashes scattered everywhere, the place looked like it always did . . . which was pretty awful. I desperately wanted to go and try to sleep in the tiny second bedroom I called my own, but I was afraid my mother would get up for a drink in the middle of the night and slice up one of her feet on the broken glass, so I got to work. First, I picked up the biggest chunks of glass by hand. Next, I swept the medium ones into a little hand-held dustpan. Finally, I vacuumed the entire room twice to get the small shards and all the bits of cigarette. It's a good thing Mom can sleep through anything, because the glass really clinked around as it shot up into the vacuum.

When I was finished, I was too pumped up to sleep, so I turned on the TV, which had suddenly shown up in our living room one miraculous night when my mom said it had "fallen off a truck." I put the first Captain America movie into our ancient DVD player. I watched the whole thing, followed by the original *Spider-Man*. I loved both of those so much, because they're about wimpy little guys who transform into superpowered crime fighters, and then battle for justice.

As for me, I'd have settled for transforming into a guy who could actually make a sound in the face of evil. Or a guy who could reach the kitchen faucet without a step stool.

When I climbed into bed, I couldn't shut my mind off. I kept picturing Johnny's face and hearing his words. He wouldn't have talked to me like that if my father had still been alive.

Of course, if my father had been alive, I wouldn't have ever had to worry about my mom's long string of losers. Or my mom's drinking. Or our money issues. Or anything.

As far as I could figure it, anybody with two parents had nothing in the world to complain about. It was a little hard to be sure, though. I hadn't had a father since I was three. All I even had to remember him by was a cheap little plastic sheriff's star he had bought me at a beachside souvenir shop on the last day I had ever spent with him. I vaguely remembered that I had been angry about something, and he'd gotten me the star to cheer me up.

I was sick of all of my problems. But mostly I was sick of feeling afraid. Spider-Man hadn't been afraid after he got his powers. Captain America had been fearless even when he was a weakling—that's why he was chosen for the super-soldier treatment that made him a superhero.

Maybe it was the stress of the evening. Maybe it was the fact that sixth grade seemed like a chance for a new start. Maybe I was just going nuts. But I came up with a wacky idea: I was going to be like Spider-Man and Captain America. I was going to do good deeds, right wrongs, stand up against evil, and protect anybody who was smaller or weaker than I was.

Assuming I could *find* anybody smaller or weaker than I was.

I didn't fall asleep until around three a.m., and then my hamster woke me at six by shuffling around his glass tank and munching on seeds. He basically functioned as an organic alarm clock—and it was a good thing, because my mom was certainly *not* a morning person. I actually kept Freddy in her room, because she wasn't allergic to him like I was, but he never woke her up. Meanwhile, I could always hear Freddy, no matter where I was in the apartment. I forced myself out of bed, went into Mom's room, and sprinkled some seed mix into Freddy's bowl. Mom never stopped snoring.

Then I got ready for school alone in the dark.

I didn't really mind. I was used to it, and when you're alone, at least nobody is bothering you. The only bummer was when I looked in the fridge for food and realized Mom hadn't gotten any. Apparently, her last check had been spent on other things.

Way in the back of the very top kitchen cabinet (which I could reach only by climbing on top of the peeling Formica countertop), I found an ancient tube of crackers.

Was it any wonder I didn't grow? I was pretty sure that at that very moment, in the rich-kid mansions across town, my archenemy, Bowen Gregory Strack, and his travel-soccer-playing minions were all washing down their third bowls of sugary cereal with fresh berries and cream.

I had heard of fresh berries and cream. Fresh berries and cream sounded awesome. Fresh *anything* sounded awesome. We never had fresh food in our house. Or even cooked food.

The only time my mom lit a stove burner was when she ran out of matches and needed to fire up a cigarette.

I must have started to doze off a couple of times while I was doing my bathroom stuff, because the next thing I knew, it was time to run out and catch the school bus. I grabbed my backpack with the two patched-up holes in one side where pencils had stabbed through, shoved on my worn-out Goodwill sneakers, and headed for the door.

At the last minute, something made me run back to my room, grab my dad's sheriff's star, and shove it down into the left front pocket of my jeans.

In the bright sunlight at the bus stop, I noticed that my jeans had a big stain on one leg from kneeling in ashes, but I didn't have time to run back and change. Come to think of it, I didn't have another pair, anyway. Thank goodness it was only going to be a half day, because I was a sleepy, stained wreck.

As soon as we got to school, the entire sixth grade was herded into the auditorium by a bunch of teachers with bull-horns. Because nothing says "Welcome to your new school!" like a bunch of people frantically shouting at you and driving you into an enclosed space. I had seen enough TV documentaries about cattle drives to know that these kinds of scenes didn't usually end well.

Inside the auditorium, which smelled like moldy old socks, there was complete chaos, as every homeroom teacher was reading as loudly as humanly possible from a list of names in order to separate us by class. I was wondering what super genius had devised this so-called system when I suddenly heard an ancient, bent-over old lady croak my name: "Maverick Falconer! Maverick Falconer!" I got in line in front of her. After a few minutes, when the whole grade had basically been sorted out, a booming, rumbly voice from the front ordered us to follow our teachers and be seated. Then, as soon as every butt was in a chair, the guy onstage (who was a blur to me, because I was in desperate need of eyeglasses) started reaming us out.

"Sixth graders, that is NOT how we enter an auditorium at Montvale West Middle School."

I was like, *Well, umm . . . apparently, that is* exactly *how we enter an auditorium at Montvale West Middle School.*

"At Montvale West, we enter quietly."

Except for all the people with the bullhorns.

"We find a seat quickly."

Right after our teachers finish sorting all four hundred of us into groups of thirty-four by reading their class lists aloud all at once.

"And then we show proper respect to our assistant principal!"

Well, sure. If we knew who the heck that was.

"Because *I* am your assistant principal! My name is Mr. Thomas Overbye. You may not call me *The Bee*, so don't even think about it. You may call me *Mr. Overbye* or *Sir*."

I had heard of this man. Everyone knew *The Bee*. In all three of the district's elementary schools, students whispered his name and then fainted in abject terror. Mothers used his name to frighten small children into doing their chores. Wherever evil assistant principals met and mingled, his name was whispered in awed, worshipful tones.

"Your teachers will go over the school rules and expectations with you in class. But here is what they won't say, because they shouldn't have to: We run on a system of honesty, respect, and order. If you are honest, treat others with respect, and behave in an orderly manner, you won't have to deal with me.

"Because you. Do. Not. Want. To. Deal. With. Me!

"Oh, and one other thing: Our goal is to turn you into self-motivated, lifelong learners who can think for yourselves. But that can only happen if you listen to your elders, do exactly as you're told, and work hard to pass your statewide tests each year."

Right. So in order to become lifelong thinkers, all we have to do is stop thinking for ourselves for the next three years. I'm feeling better and better about this place by the minute.

Once we were all thoroughly horrified and depressed, The Bee ordered our teachers to march us to homeroom. The last thing he said to our whole grade was that each of us should do our very best to stay out of his office for the next three years.

I tried to follow The Bee's command. Honestly. But somehow, I missed by two years, three hundred sixty-four days, twenty-three hours, and forty-six minutes.

Eggs on Toast, without the Eggs

On the way out of the auditorium I was pretty nervous, so I tried to calm myself down by thinking about the one thing I did have going for me in this hard, cruel world: a walking, talking "Get Out of Jail Free" card. Her name is Catherine, but I just call her Aunt Cat. She's my dad's younger sister, and she is also the only person in the world I can totally depend on.

I don't get to see my aunt super often, because she and my mom haven't gotten along since one day two years ago, when my mom did something really bad. Still, when I do see Aunt Cat, it's great. Usually, she swings by my apartment to pick me up when my mom is at work. I've never exactly been able to figure out how, but Aunt Cat always seems to know what shift my mother is working. That is a very good thing as far as I'm concerned, because the less I have to stand around and watch my only two adult relatives square off and hiss at each other, the better.

Anyway, my aunt is good at almost everything. She has a tiny, bright yellow, two-seater stick-shift car with an incredibly great stereo, and she can drive it in traffic at, like, seventy miles per hour while she talks on the phone, eats a muffin, drinks coffee, and changes radio stations. She's a hairstylist, and I have seen her dye one person's hair, give another person a wash and cut, and answer the phone, while supervising a new employee at the same time. My mom once told me that Aunt Cat has been living on her own since she was seventeen. She's incredibly hyper, but she never messes anything up.

Well, except for anything involving food preparation. If I happen to be at her apartment during mealtime, she will always ask me what I want. So I will ask her what she has. Then she will say, "How about a ham and cheese sandwich?"

But when she starts looking in her fridge, she will add, "But . . . um . . . the vegetarian kind?"

Or she will offer me her famous specialty: eggs on toast, without the eggs. Once, when her bread turned out to be moldy, we were left with eggs on toast, without the eggs or the toast. Which meant our dinner was peanut butter straight out of the jar, licked directly from our spoons.

Actually, the fact that she had two clean spoons kind of impressed me.

But the dining aspects of our relationship don't really matter. What does matter to me, more than anything, is what Aunt Cat said to me at the end of the disastrous summer incident two years ago. She was about to get in her car in front of my apartment after my mom had screamed and yelled at her to go away. I was crying so hard I could barely get a breath, but I managed to ask, "Will I still see you?"

Aunt Cat knelt down so her face was level with mine, grabbed both of my shoulders, stared into my eyes, and said, "Maverick, buddy, if you need me, call me. I don't care what's happening. I don't care what kind of trouble you're in. I don't care what I have going on. I will drop everything and come to you."

The Deadly Art of Locker Karate

As I arrived at the doorway of my first class, I told myself I wasn't going to need Aunt Cat anytime soon. I was like, *How hard can this be? What kind of terrible situation can I possibly get myself into on the first half day of school?*

Besides, the class was homeroom. Who gets in trouble in homeroom?

This guy.

My homeroom teacher's name, which I hadn't caught during the assembly, was Mrs. Sakofsky. She called each student up to her desk individually, handed us a little paper with our locker combination printed on it, and told us to go out in the hallway and open up our locker a few times, until we got the hang of it. When I got out there and found my locker, I couldn't believe my luck: I was right between Jamie Thompson and Bowen Gregory Strack. Perfect! My two greatest foes in one convenient location!

I almost stormed back in there and demanded a different locker. I mean, what kind of system puts kids with the last names Thompson, Falconer, and Strack in a row?

"Oh, look," Jamie said in her fake-sweet voice. "It's Maverick Falconer. Mavvy, did you bring the other six dwarves?"

"Hey, what's up?" I said. Even when Jamie's being obnoxious, I always try to be friendly.

"Everything, compared to you," Jamie replied.

I wasn't going to let her childish insults bring me down to her level. Metaphorically, I mean. Physically, she towered over me. I had to crane my neck to see anything above her chin.

I smiled at her, hoping she would sense how bad I still felt about the Great Three-Legged Fiasco.

"What are you looking at?" she snarled. "Are you actually checking out my front teeth—you, of all people?"

"No! Of course not! I would never look at your front teeth. Um, I mean, not that there's anything wrong with them or anything. The dentists did a beautiful job!" *Oh, shoot me*, I thought.

"Thanks," she hissed. "That's very flattering. Of course, I wouldn't have needed hours of painful mouth surgery if you weren't the clumsiest kid on the entire planet!"

All righty, then.

I stepped between Jamie and Bowen and squinted at my paper, because the numbers on it were pretty small. Like I said, I needed glasses, but my mom isn't big on things like making eye doctor appointments. She's not even *small* on things like eye doctor appointments. The only way I was going to get my eyes checked was if I accidentally impaled one of them on a lawn dart or something.

Anyway, Bowen said, "Check this out!" and banged his locker with the side of one huge, hamlike fist. His locker sprang open. It was like magic. Bowen might have been, like, the Elvis of spoiled, pretty-boy rich jocks—but I had to admit he had style.

"Wow, that's cool!" Jamie purred. Jamie didn't even *like* Bowen, but she knew how much I despised him.

"I can do that," I said, without thinking. Because, you know, I couldn't. I had never even opened a locker using the combination.

"Go for it," Bowen said. "Just remember, the key is to hit it in *exactly* the right spot. You have to become one with the lock mechanism!"

What kind of mystical Jedi ninja party-magician trick was this? *Become one with the lock mechanism?* Sheesh!

I took a deep breath, blew on the edge of my hand, and hit my locker the way Bowen had, a couple of inches above the spinning black dial.

Nothing happened.

Wait, no—*something* happened. The locker rang like a gong and involuntary tears of pain sprang to my eyes.

"I guess you just don't have the touch," Bowen said as he closed his locker. I could hear the laughter in his voice.

I gritted my teeth. If Bowen Gregory Strack could do it, I didn't see any reason why I couldn't.

"I'm just warming up," I hissed.

Then I whacked the locker again, harder.

All I got was more tears and a louder noise.

SPANG!

Jamie said, "Too bad that lock isn't made out of teeth. You'd have it busted open in no time!" I turned to her and tried to think of a witty retort, resisting with all my will-power the urge to clasp my hand and scream. As she and I stared into each other's eyes, I heard another gentle *clink* behind me. I whirled, and saw Bowen blow on his knuckles again as he swung his reopened locker shut.

"Don't feel too bad," he said. "Maybe you can't get the right angle from way down there." Then he walked away, back into homeroom.

Jamie seemed to think this was the funniest thing in the world. I did not.

When Jamie and every other kid in the class had gone back into the room and I was completely alone in the hallway, I gave my hardest punch yet. Needless to say, the locker didn't open.

This was too much.

I snapped and started pounding on the thing with both fists. I pretended it was Bowen's face. Or Johnny's. Or the face of any of my mom's other abusive loser boyfriends. I punched and punched until I had to stop because my knuckles were bleeding and I was out of breath.

That was when I noticed that it had gotten kind of dark in the hall.

A massive hand tapped me on the shoulder. I whirled and literally banged into the protruding stomach of the largest man I had ever seen in my life. He had to be at least six and a half feet tall, with super-broad shoulders, that big belly, a bushy red handlebar mustache, and wild red hair. If Santa Claus had married a Viking queen, their firstborn son would have looked like this dude.

"Interesting tactic," he rumbled.

Holy cow! I knew that voice! I was standing face-to-belly with Mr. Overbye!

"I generally use the combination method myself," he said. Then he turned and started walking away down the hall. I could have sworn the floor actually trembled each time one of his feet landed.

"Coming?" he asked.

Somehow I knew it wasn't really a question.

The Bird and The Bee

A couple of very tense minutes later, I was sitting on a very hard chair in the school office, right next to Mr. Overbye's desk, staring down at my oozing knuckles.

I was dead. I was *so* dead.

I was a tiny bit afraid I might wet myself.

Then The Bee spoke, boomingly. **"The Fist Trick."**

"Um, excuse me?" I said. Then I added, "Sir?" I had no idea what he was talking about, but I thought being as polite as possible might help keep me alive a little while longer. Mr. Overbye looked up over my head for a few seconds, then sighed and began speaking again, much more softly.

"You fell for the Fist Trick. It happens to at least one sixth grader every year. The way it works is, an older student

23

dials in all three numbers of his locker combination, but doesn't actually pull the locker open after the third number. Then he hits the locker just above the dial, and it seems to pop open by magic. Does this sound rather *familiar* to you? Did an older student hit his locker and make it pop open, then challenge you to do the same thing?"

"Uh, not an *older* kid."

The Bee's eyes flicked up and over me again. Then he leaned toward me by lacing his hands together and placing his chin on top of them.

"So who was it?" he asked. His voice was almost a whisper.

"A kid in my class. Just a kid."

"Does that kid happen to have older siblings who have attended this school?"

I nodded. Bowen had a big sister. I guessed she'd told him about the stupid locker trick.

"But you don't want to tell me his name?"

I shook my head.

"Because you don't want to be a tattletale?"

"No, sir, I don't." I wanted Bowen Gregory Strack to suffer, but *I* wanted to be the one to make him suffer—personally.

"Well, I can respect that . . . for now." He sat up straight. "BUT. If this young man continues to harass you, I want to know about it. Do you understand?"

I nodded. My neck sure was getting a good workout.

"Listen, son. This school can be an easy place or a hard place." He smiled at me in what he might have thought was a reassuring way. But considering that his mouth was wider than my entire head, the effect was mostly just terrifying. "You can make it easy by just staying out of this office. And you do that by using some common sense. Think before you act. Say to yourself, 'Is this a smart move, or a dumb move?' Do you think you can try to do that?"

I nodded yet again.

"Because here's one last tip: Punching metal is always going to be a dumb move. When you throw yourself up against something harder than you are, that never goes well. Now, I am going to write you a pass to see the nurse before you go back to class. Her name is Mrs. Vogler."

I sat up a little straighter and breathed a sigh of relief. For someone with his reputation, The Bee hadn't been so ultra-terrible. I mean, his randomly changing voice volume was odd, but assistant principals were *supposed* to be odd. I was starting to believe I might be safe.

Apparently, The Bee had a part-time job as a mind reader at a circus somewhere, because he said, "Oh, don't think you're out of the woods yet, kid. I know what students tell each other about me. But Mrs. Vogler is scarier than I could ever hope to be."

I walked to the nurse's office, only getting lost twice on the way. When I got there, I kind of craned my neck nervously around one edge of the door frame.

All I saw was a teensy-weensy old lady sitting at a desk, humming a show tune and nibbling from a bag of trail mix. She didn't look alarming at all. She reminded me of a mouse, or a chipmunk, or a sweet little . . .

Bird.

Holy cow, I knew who this was. She was the other most frightening staff member in the building. If The Bee was the world's scariest assistant principal, The Bird was the world's scariest school employee, period. She had been working at the middle school since the dawn of time, and apparently, her nursing methods were as primitive as you might expect from someone whose earliest patients had probably been carried in on the backs of woolly mammoths. It was just my luck that I had to run into The Bee and The Bird on my first day.

I had to get away from there before she noticed me.

"Come in?" she said. Somehow it sounded like a question. Well, like a question would sound if you played it on a tiny wooden flute.

It was too late to escape.

She asked me my name, read Mr. Overbye's note, and leaned close to examine my injured hands. Then she straightened back up and said, "We'll have those cleaned up in a jiffy?" Apparently, everything this woman said sounded like a question.

She bustled away into a little supply room and came back with a dusty-looking box that read GAUZE PADS on the side in huge block letters, and a spray can of Lysol.

"Hold out your hands, please?" she said.

Without thinking, I did. Then, before I could react, she sprayed the open wounds with the Lysol. I yelped like a coyote on fire.

"Oh, dear!" The Bird said. "I don't think this is the spray I meant to use? I really need to find my reading glasses before I kill somebody . . . again? But as long as it stings, that probably means it did the trick, right? And all's well that ends well, I always say."

Then she smiled innocently, wrapped my knuckles in

27

about an inch of gauze, and sent me on my way. Before I even got out the door, she was already humming and munching again.

I was pretty sure the tune was "He's Got the Whole World in His Hands."

The Trash Can Tango

Well, I almost made it to my third-period class. With the half-day schedule, I had already missed science and math, but I had a real shot at being on time for social studies until I went charging around a corner and found myself heading straight at Bowen.

Swell.

He was about ten feet away from me with a bunch of his soccer friends. I knew they were his soccer friends because they were all wearing matching black warm-up jackets. It was pretty intimidating when the whole team came at you in a crowded corridor sporting their gear, which also featured two bright yellow letters inside of an oval on the back and one side of the chest: MU. The letters stood for Montvale United. Montvale was the name of our town.

Actually, the letters were the reason Bowen hated me in the first place. Way back in third grade, when their travel team first formed, all of those guys were in my class—along with Jamie. Yup, third grade had ended up being a real standout year.

One day, they all showed up wearing MU T-shirts. So I walked up to Bowen at recess and asked, "Why does your shirt say 'Moo'?"

He got mad and said, "Can't you read? It says M-U!"

I said, "Of course I can read! That spells 'Moo'! I just want to know why you are all wearing 'Moo' shirts. Is it some kind of cow holiday?"

I wasn't making fun of him or anything. What did I know about his stupid travel soccer wear? I had to drop out of T-ball in first grade when my mom drank up the fifteen-dollar T-shirt fee.

But Bowen got even madder, put me in a headlock, and told me he wouldn't let me out until I screamed "MOO!" at the top of my lungs. His exact words were, "I'll teach you to say 'Moo!'" I was like, *I thought you were trying to teach me not to say "Moo!"*

One thing led to another, and we ended up wrestling around on the smelly blacktop next to the Dumpster. His shirt got rotting school-lunch taco meat all over it, and after one of the lunch monitors finally broke us up, I saw that Bowen's nose was bleeding.

Back then, Bowen and I had been the same size. It seemed almost unbelievable looking back, but Bowen had been tied with me for the title of Smallest Kid in Third Grade. By fourth grade, he had been somewhere in between smallest and biggest, and by the end of fifth, he had been so huge that he had become his soccer team's full-time goalie. Apparently, all he had to do was stand in the goal, and 90 percent of the shots were blocked by his massive body.

Off the field, Bowen preferred playing offense. Like right now, he was holding some smaller kid's math book up over his head. The little guy, who was probably still taller than me, was jumping up, trying to reach the book, while the whole soccer team laughed. It *did* look ridiculous, because the kid's hand wasn't even getting close.

I stood there, trying to stare a hole in Bowen's forehead.

Bowen growled at me. "What are you looking at?"

I swallowed. Obviously, I was looking at Bowen. But now everyone else in the entire hallway was looking straight at *me*. I had to do something, but my whole body was frozen yet again.

Luckily, my mouth still worked.

"Just give him his book, Bowen," I said.

"Or what? Are you going to jump up and punch me in the knee?"

For a split second, I might have considered The Bee's words: *Is this a smart move or a dumb move?* But it didn't matter.

Maybe it was the trick Bowen had already played on me that morning. Maybe it was the way he was teasing the other boy. Maybe it was the words he had used—the exact same words Johnny had said to me after he had hit my mother. Maybe it was the tone of his voice—that same superior, mocking tone I'd been hearing over and over for years.

Whatever it was, something set me off.

There's no nice way to describe what happened next. I went nuts. I dropped my book bag, put my head down, and charged at Bowen. His team scattered like bowling pins—mostly from the sheer shock of my crazed attack. I felt a slight impact against my right shoulder, and then heard a *CLANG!* Too late, I dimly realized I had just knocked the little guy into a row of lockers.

Oops.

A split second later, my head and shoulders slammed into Bowen, who started to exclaim, "What—"

Then he stepped away from me, and the backs of his legs hit the lip of one of those huge garbage cans that custodians use when they're emptying a whole hallway of classroom trash baskets. There was no way I was strong enough to knock Bowen over, but unfortunately for him, he started to lose his grip on the math book he was holding over his head, and leaned back to hold on to it.

Wha-BAM! In he tumbled.

Everybody in the hall froze in horror, including me. I have to admit I felt a brief thrill of victory, but of course I knew that Bowen was going to kill me when he climbed back out of the garbage.

Well, as soon as he got what appeared to be, um, a half-eaten banana off his head.

Bowen roared.

And then an answering roar, much louder, came from immediately behind my left ear: **"What—is—going—on—here???"**

You know those school administrators who just sit around in their offices all day, playing on their computers? Just my luck—apparently, The Bee wasn't one of them.

Because when I turned around, his mustache brushed against the top of my head. It was alarming, disgusting, and just the slightest bit tickly.

This time, The Bee didn't bother asking whether I was coming along to his office. I already knew the drill.

Or Rather, the Trash Can Ballet

I spent most of the next twenty minutes sitting on a hard chair in the office. After a little while, the small kid I had inadvertently body-slammed came in with an ice pack pressed to the side of his head. He was wincing, and reeked of Lysol. Both he and the nearest secretary kept shooting me evil glares every few seconds. Great! The office staff already thought I was a bad kid, and I had made a brand-new enemy.

And I still hadn't even set foot in an actual class. At this rate, I would probably get into the *Guinness Book of World Records*. I couldn't stand it. I turned to the kid.

"So, um, hey."

He looked at me like I was something that had just dripped on his shoe from a lunch lady's glop ladle. I didn't let it stop me. "Sorry about the . . . well, the smashing-you-into-the-locker thing. I was just trying to help you out."

He sneered at me. "Ah, you were trying to *help me out*. What do you do when you're trying to save somebody's life—blast their face with a blowtorch?"

"Mistakes were made, okay?"

He turned up his nose and said, "Clearly."

Then we sat in icy silence until The Bee's door opened, and Bowen slunk out, looking like he had just sweated his way through a horrible ordeal. When he got close enough for me to smell the essence of banana coming off his hair, he hissed, "We were dancing! Got that?"

What was he trying to tell me? And why? Was it a warning? Was The Bee some kind of sicko who liked to dance with sixth graders? He hadn't tried any disco moves with me before, so it seemed unlikely.

I didn't have much time to wonder, because The Bee immediately called me into his office. As soon as I was seated, he said, "Long time no see."

Yay! An assistant principal who was also an amateur comedian. VERY amateur.

"Never," he continued, "in my twenty-three years in this district, have I seen two students—two *sixth graders*—cause so much trouble so early in the school year. If this is what you do during your first morning here, I shudder to imagine what you will do when we have a full day! Now, would you mind telling me what you and Mr. Strack were doing in that hallway?"

Bowen's face flashed in my mind. Suddenly, I thought I understood what he had been trying to tell me. "Would you believe we were dancing?"

The Bee looked above my head, then sat back in his chair, folded his hands on his tummy, and grinned mischievously. "Really?" he said.

"Yes, sir. We take a dance class together. You know, after school. And, uh, on weekends. Sometimes."

"And what kind of dance class would this happen to be?"

Crud. Bowen really needed to practice whispering faster. "Um, hip-hop?"

"Nice try, Maverick."

"Well, sure, the end of the routine clearly needs some work, but—"

"No, I said 'nice try' because Mr. Strack told me you were both involved with the study of the noble art of ballet."

Ballet? I thought. *Seriously, Bowen?*

"Yes, ballet," I said.

"Can you please list four ballet positions for me? Surely your ballet studies have taught you the basics?"

"Well, there's the leap. Then the . . . jump. And the . . . backflip?"

"Mr. Strack couldn't name any, either. The next time you both decide to lie, I suggest you do your research first."

Mr. Overbye went on to tell me he would let me know about my punishment later. Then he sent me back to class and called in the other kid, whose name turned out to be Nathan Something-or-other.

Based on the look Nathan gave me, I suspected he would be more than happy to give The Bee some punishment suggestions.

I actually spent nearly seventeen minutes in my sixth-period class, which was English with an extremely odd man named Mr. Kurt. When I came in late and handed him my note, he said, "Right-o-rooney, Mr. Falconer! Just take the open seat at the back table over there and get ready to make some beauty! We're working on life collages. All you have to do is arrange some pictures into a visually pleasing pattern that tells us a story about *you*."

Naturally, Mr. Kurt had put me next to the other person who had come in late: Bowen. Like everyone else, he was already cutting out his pictures. Typical Bowen Strack—his stacked photos were all either famous athletes, or close-ups of dollar signs or actual money.

Bowen was a really deep thinker.

"Ballet? Who takes ballet?" I hissed at him, grabbing an old magazine and starting to flip through it randomly.

"What?" he said. "I could take ballet. I happen to be extremely graceful. And flexible. In fact, my elbows and knees are double jointed. Check this ou—"

"Dudesters! Work!" barked Mr. Kurt.

I grabbed a pair of scissors and slashed furiously around an image of a United States Army soldier in full desert gear. Well, as furiously as one can slash with pink plastic school scissors. "I don't care if you're double jointed. You couldn't answer any of The Bee's questions about ballet. Plus, I told The Bee we took hip-hop. Now we're busted!"

"Hip-hop? Like *you're* coordinated enough for hip-hop!" Bowen snipped out a bunch of random-seeming letters from advertisements, and then rearranged them on the table to read GET PAID. I wanted to vomit. Instead, I focused on finding pictures that said something about my life. Of course, if I had been totally honest, I would have cut out a pile of vodka bottles, and maybe glued down a bunch of dollar bills with Xs drawn over them. Instead, I found a picture of Sheriff Woody from *Toy Story*, and cut out his badge. Next,

I stumbled upon a whole double-page spread advertising a Marvel Comics DVD collection, so I grabbed images of Spider-Man and Captain America. Finally, I looked through a huge stack of *National Geographic*s until I located a map of Afghanistan.

With a huge lump forming in my throat, I cut—super carefully—around the outline of the map.

Mr. Kurt cleared his throat and announced, "All righty, little artisans, you need to start assembling now! Just remember what I told you about this new glue that the school ordered, okay?"

Everyone started laying out their pictures on pieces of poster board. I leaned toward Bowen and asked what we were supposed to remember about the new glue.

"Oh," he said, smiling in an unusually friendly way, "it's finger glue. You just dab it onto the back of each picture with your fingertips and then stick the picture right onto the paper. It's supposed to be better for the environment than the old glue sticks, because you only need a teeny-tiny bit of it."

"Thanks," I said, grabbing one of the little glue bottles from the tabletop. I turned the picture of Captain America upside down, squeezed the littlest drop possible onto my index finger, and touched the back of the picture. Instantly, it stuck to my finger.

Bowen giggled.

I couldn't believe it. He had gotten me twice in one day!

"Bowen!" I practically yelled.

Mr. Kurt said, "What are you doing at that table? Do I have to come back there or something, pals?"

"Sorry, sir," Bowen said. "We're just bonding!" Then he added, under his breath, "Darn. I *knew* it was either finger glue or instant-hardening superglue. I always get those confused."

Just then, the intercom blared to life:

"PLEASE SEND MAVERICK FALCONER TO THE OFFICE. WITH HIS THINGS."

Naturally, the whole class made the "*oooo-ooo*" noise that everyone always makes when somebody gets called to the office. Then they stared at me as I frantically snipped away as much of the picture from around my finger as I could and grabbed my bag.

"Don't worry about your collage materials, buddy-rooney," Mr. Kurt said, in what seemed like a sort of sympathetic tone. "Your friend Mr. Strack can put them in a folder for you. Right, Bowen-boy?"

"With pleasure!"

I'm sure, I thought as I left the room. It was hard not to feel sorry for myself as I trudged toward the office—again—with the backs of my hands wrapped in gauze, a lengthening criminal record, and the decapitated head of Captain America permanently glued to my fingertip.

A Meeting with Mom

Around the corner from the office, I passed Nathan, who stared straight down at the floor the whole time. Either he was avoiding eye contact or he really, really admired the school's swirly, poop-brown floor tiles.

The instant my butt hit the seat in The Bee's office, I knew why Nathan had been looking down. He had told on me. Now, instead of The Bee thinking I was a victim who was reluctant to name names—which had actually been true—he thought I was some kind of improbable mega-bully.

"So," he said in a dangerously cheerful tone, "Nathan just finished telling me about your human bowling exploits in the hallway."

Human bowling? Huh?

"I wouldn't have thought a little guy like you could take out an entire soccer team, plus an innocent bystander, with one charge, but then again, my five-year-old daughter once rolled a strike with a six-pound ball at Lizzy Lavinsky's birthday party, and I wouldn't have believed *that* if I hadn't seen it, either."

I sat and stared at him. Had he just accused me of charging into an entire soccer team and scattering them like bowling pins? That was so . . . so . . . so . . .

Technically accurate. Dang.

And then, had he also compared me to a six-pound bowling ball rolled by a five-year-old girl? Argh. Again, he sort of had a point. I curled my hands into fists, because when I glanced down into my lap, it had momentarily looked like Captain America was laughing at me.

"Well, do you have anything to say for yourself? Anything else you'd like me to know about your foray into the beautiful, yet strangely violent, art of dance?"

I didn't say a word. What good would it have done?

Mr. Overbye pushed his phone across the desk to me and uttered the three most frightening words in the English language: "Call your mother." Then he told me she needed to come and get me. Apparently, my brief experience with scissors and glue was going to be it for me in terms of first-day academics.

I didn't know what to do. My mom couldn't come.

She didn't have a car.

She was probably hungover.

Or still sleeping.

Or, worst of all, drunk again.

She would either have to walk three miles or take two different buses to reach the school. I knew she didn't have the money for a taxi. Plus, her face probably looked awful; the swelling was always much worse the day after.

I almost started to cry, but stopped myself by reaching into my jeans pocket and rubbing my dad's star. I didn't remember much about my father, but I thought I remembered him saying to me once that sheriffs didn't cry in public.

"I'm waiting," Mr. Overbye said.

I thought and thought. I rubbed my star and squinched my eyes shut as tightly as I could. Then I said a little prayer and punched ten digits with the Captain's face. As soon as I heard a voice on the other end, I blurted out, "Mom, can you please come get me at the middle school? Uh, Montvale West, of course. Very funny, Mom . . . In the office? Right now? I got in trouble. *Yes*, this is Maverick. Who else would it be?"

I rolled my eyes at The Bee, as if to say, *Mothers!*

I said two more words into the phone: "Please hurry!" Then I hung up before Mr. Overbye could try to get in on the conversation.

The Bee sent me out into the main office to wait, which was a good thing, because I hadn't actually called my mother. Once, Aunt Cat had made me memorize her number in case of an emergency. But ever since the time my mom flipped out on her, I had never called my aunt in a crisis. Today, though, I had given in. It was a pretty big risk, because Cat was as wild as her name, but I figured nothing could be as awful as having my new assistant principal meet my actual mess of a mother.

Still, I was going to have to do an awful lot of explaining, awfully fast, the instant Aunt Cat walked in.

Or stormed in, as it turned out. Aunt Cat knew how to make an entrance. First of all, she was really tall—probably about five eight without the super-high heels she was wearing. Second, she had ultra-bright pink hair. Third, she was dressed in a leopard-print pantsuit and a short fake-fur coat. Aunt Cat has a pretty unique sense of style.

Anyway, she shoved the door open so hard it clanged off the coatrack behind it, while her head swiveled until her eyes locked on mine. She closed the distance between us in three long strides and enveloped me in an extremely bone-crushing hug.

One of the secretaries had leaped up and was saying, "Excuse me, miss," but Aunt Cat waved her away over my shoulder. At the same time, she snarled into my ear, "What's going on, Mav?"

"I got in a fight."

"A *fight*? You?"

At the sight of my aunt—the only person in the whole world who made me feel safe—I had immediately started crying. This made it hard to speak, so I nodded against her shoulder.

"Did you win?"

I managed to choke out, "Sort of."

"How do you *sort of* win a fight?"

I took a deep breath. "Well, I knocked the other guy into a garbage can, and then a banana peel got stuck in his hair, but I accidentally smashed another kid's head into a locker, and that kid told on me."

She pushed me away and held me at arm's length. "A banana peel?" she asked. Then she noticed the gauze on my hands and the head of Captain America on my fingertip, shook her head, and started giggling. "A banana peel? Only *you*, Maverick Falconer . . ."

Just then, a voice rumbled from behind me. "Excuse me, Mrs. Falconer, but we need to talk about your son's behavior."

Aunt Cat squeezed my wrists, winked at me, then whirled to face The Bee. I crossed my fingers.

"Yes," she said through clenched teeth, "we do!"

In his office, The Bee went through his version of my whole day, while Aunt Cat nodded solemnly at all the right times. As soon as he finished, she turned to me and said, "Young man, I hope you understand the seriousness of all this. I am sure Mr. Overbye here has better things to do with his time than handle your messes all day. Do you understand me?"

I nodded. Boy, she was a really good actress. Either that, or her moods changed extremely fast.

"If I have to come down here again, Maverick David Falconer, you are going to be one extremely unhappy little sixth grader. Now, you are going to go straight to your room when you get home and think about what you've done." She turned and looked sweetly at The Bee. She might have batted her eyelashes at him. He might even have blushed, but maybe—hopefully—I was imagining that part. "Don't you worry, Mr. Overbye. Between us, I'm sure we can get

Maverick straightened out. You have my number if you, um, need to get in touch."

Then she stood, gestured for me to follow, and strode out of there, pausing just long enough to wave over her shoulder at The Bee.

She didn't start giggling again until we got to the street.

Heroes and Hamsters

By the time we got in her car, Aunt Cat had stopped laughing. First, she asked why I had called her instead of my mother. I mumbled something about a job, although I may have neglected to mention the fact that my mom was busy *looking for* a job.

Next, Aunt Cat started in on my behavior. "Maverick," she said, "what were you thinking? A fight? Against an entire soccer team? In front of a hallway full of witnesses? On the first day of school? In what universe could that ever seem like a good idea?"

I could feel my face flush. "I wasn't trying to get in a fight! But there's this one kid named Bowen Strack—"

"Banana Boy?"

"Yeah, him. Anyway, he thinks he's so great because he's rich and popular and everything. But he's mean! And he tricked me into punching my locker."

"So that was your first trip to the office, right?"

"Right. And then I was walking to my next class, minding my own business, when—"

"He attacked you? Why didn't you say something to Mr. Overbye, then?"

"Well, um, actually, *I* attacked *him*."

She looked at me like my face had just turned purple, with hot-pink polka dots. "You attacked him? Randomly? You just jumped him, out of the blue?"

"Not exactly. He was with all his rich, stupid, mean soccer friends. And he had taken a book away from some new kid named Nate, who's small like me. So I looked at Bowen really hard. That's all I did—I just stared at him. I thought maybe he would stop torturing the kid if he knew someone besides his group of idiots was watching. Then he said something and I kind of lost it."

I looked down at my hands. There was dumb old Captain America, grinning up from my fingertip like this was all some big joke. I was starting to hate that guy.

Aunt Cat's voice was much gentler as she asked, "What did he say, Mav? Did he make fun of you?"

My throat felt kind of hot and closed, like I was going to cry again if I tried to talk, so I just sat there like a fool, until Aunt Cat reached across the seat of the car and began stroking my hair. Then I actually did start sobbing.

I'm pretty sure that's not how superheroes roll.

When I finally got myself under control, I said, "No, he didn't make fun of me, exactly. He kind of . . . challenged me."

Aunt Cat sighed. "Oh, kid. If you start swinging every time some knucklehead challenges you, I'm going to be getting a lot of phone calls."

"But what was I supposed to do, ignore him? He was picking on somebody smaller than him."

"I know, but—"

"Aunt Cat, what would my dad have done?"

She kind of jerked back from me. I never talked about my father in front of her. I basically never talked about him in front of anyone, but one of my earliest memories was of her crying on the freshly turned earth at the foot of his grave, so she would normally have been the last person in the world with whom I'd have brought this up.

But then she smiled. "Maverick, your dad would have fed that kid his teeth, one by one."

I felt some kind of frozen lump in my chest crack open, just a bit.

"Aunt Cat, is it true that he was a hero? I mean, a real hero?"

She leaned back in her seat and sighed. "Well, you know how he died . . . That was pretty heroic. Nobody signs up to be a military firefighter unless he's *some* kind of special, right?"

I nodded.

"And I don't think you ever knew this, but your father was paying my way through college until he died. Then I had to drop out and go to beauty school, because it was cheaper and faster. Whatever. I guess what I'm trying to say is that he was *my* hero. He was my big brother, and he always, always watched out for me. When I lost him, it was like losing a guardian angel. But . . ."

"But what?"

Really quickly, Aunt Cat sat up straight, started the car, and slammed it into gear. Just before she stomped her high-heeled foot down on the gas pedal, I could have sworn she wiped a tear away from under one eye.

"But nothing. I just noticed the time. Geez, I have a client in fifteen minutes! You're going to have to explain all of this to your mother. Do you promise?"

"I promise."

"For real?"

"For real. And, Aunt Cat? Thanks." I *would* tell my mom about the trouble I'd gotten in. I didn't say that my plan was to wait until she'd had a bunch of drinks and was about to pass out.

"You're welcome. And hey, I'll drop off some wood shavings for Freddy next week sometime, all right?"

"That's perfect! Thanks again!"

Aunt Cat was basically the reason I had Freddy in the first place. There was a pet store next to the salon where she worked, and I was pretty sure the owner, Bill, had a crush on her like every other grown-up man in the world did, so he gave her big discounts on Freddy's food and the wood shavings for the bottom of his tank. Even the tank itself and Freddy's drinking bottle and exercise wheel had been gifts from Aunt Cat, dropped off when my mother wasn't around.

But getting Freddy had been all my idea. One day after school in fourth grade, Aunt Cat had been watching me at the salon while my mom went on some kind of ridiculous job interview, and I got bored, so I went next door to stare at the hamsters for, like, the ten millionth time. I noticed this one baby hamster in the back corner of the big tank, all alone. It was scratched up and looked like it was shivering. When I scrunched my nose up to the glass, I saw that it had a bloody, raw stump where one of its front paws should be.

I stared at the little guy for a long time, until Aunt Cat tracked me down in there. She and Bill saw what I was looking at, and Bill said, "Such a shame when they turn on one of their own like that. Poor little guy's probably gonna be dead within a day or so."

I just blurted it out: "Can I have him?"

Bill told me that I was going to have to feed this hamster out of the palm of my hand because he wouldn't be able to grip nuts and seeds with his front paws. He also said I would have to dribble warm water into the hamster's mouth drop by drop, or the hamster would die of dehydration after having lost so much blood. Finally, Bill told me that the hamster probably wouldn't survive with only three paws, no matter what I did.

Aunt Cat saw the look on my face, and said, "I'll buy the accessories if you'll throw in the little rodent for free. What do you say?"

That's just who she is.

Anyway, I had just started turning my key in the lock on our apartment door when I realized something awful: Now The Bee thought Aunt Cat was my mom. That meant

I was going to have keep my actual mom away from every school-related event.

Wow. I was the only superhero whose *mom* had a secret identity.

My actual mother wasn't home. She had left a note: *Out job hunting. Hopefully I will catch one! :)*

Pretty cheerful, considering the situation.

And what had Aunt Cat really been thinking when she'd said, "But . . ."?

The first thing I did was take the wrapping off my hands and scrub away at Captain America while I was at it. I eventually came up with the idea of pouring nail polish remover over him, which worked. Sadly, it also made me scream when it ran down my hand onto one skinless knuckle, but hey, you can't have everything.

Mom came home a few hours later, happily convinced that hard times were over. She was always doing this. Every time a guy dumped her, or we got kicked out of an apartment, or she lost a job, she would somehow find a shred of good news. Then she would cling to it and ignore every other bit of reality, in order to convince herself that *this time* our lives were just about to turn around.

Sometimes, it was a new Prince Charming. But the guy never turned out to be a prince, or very charming. Other times, it was an "amazing" new apartment, with "great positive energies"—and bedbugs.

Once, it was the gleaming promise of a job delivering pizzas on a bicycle—wearing a clown suit.

Today, her friend Lisa had gotten her a middle-shift job at ShopMart, our local gigantic mega-store. Middle shift! That meant she would be working every day from the time I got home from school until after I went to bed. I hated the middle shift.

On the other hand, of course it was great that she had a job. And I did enjoy the huge meal of free sample foods she had gotten to take home after the job interview. Even better was that, in her excitement, she forgot to ask me about my day.

She hardly even drank anything; she just splashed the last dregs of the previous night's bottle into her share of the sample artificial fruit punch. It was barely enough to slow down her excited chatter. These nights didn't come very often, so I decided to sit back, keep my damaged hands under the table as much as possible, and smile a lot.

I was used to celebrating small victories.

How to Win Friends and
Influence People

Believe it or not, I didn't get in trouble for several weeks after that first day. Partly, I was terrified I'd get dragged to Mr. Overbye's office again and he would call my aunt/mom back in. I knew I had dodged a bullet there, plus with my mom's new work schedule, I basically only saw her for fifteen minutes after school, and then on weekends, so I never had to tell her about the first round of trouble.

There was no way I would get that lucky twice.

The other thing working in my favor was that Bowen was behaving himself. I guess even he was worried about The Bee. Whatever—I wasn't complaining.

I even did some secret good deeds. I routinely emptied our classroom's pencil sharpener, picked trash up off the floors, and closed open lockers as I walked through the hall-ways. It probably doesn't seem like much, but I kept think-ing about my dad's star in my pocket and feeling like I should try to do something every day to make a difference in the world.

I also started to make a friend, which hadn't happened in a long time. It was just too tricky. What if I got invited to somebody's birthday party? I would have to say no, because we couldn't afford a gift. What if the kid wanted to come over to my house, but my mom happened to be drunk that day? Or worse, what if she had a boyfriend at the apartment?

But somehow, I found myself talking every day with Nate, who sat at my table in three classes because it turned out that his last name was Ferguson—very close to Falconer. At first, I had been pretty mad at him for telling on me to The Bee—but, then again, I *had* slammed him into the lockers. So I got over it.

Besides, I almost had to talk to him. We were like the Shrimp Twins.

After the first day, our English teacher, Mr. Kurt, had reassigned all the seats alphabetically, so I got to trade Bowen for Nate. It started out kind of awkward, because Bowen had somehow managed to replace all of my collage materials with ghastly giant spiders, close-up photos of murder victims, baby dolls, and ballerina figures. Nate was very curious to know how this all fit together to tell my life story. Once I explained that Bowen had been assigned to put all my work in a folder for me, Nate caught on pretty fast.

"There's a Bowen in every school," he said. "And trust me, I've been to enough schools."

"Why?" I asked, chucking a guy hanging from a noose into the trash can on top of a tarantula, which appeared to be snacking on a ballet dancer.

"My dad used to be in the army," he said. "Now he sells top-secret technology to the military. We move around a lot, because his job is to set up new computer systems on different bases all over the country. It stinks. Everybody picks on the new kid. Especially the tiny new kid. Nobody ever wants to be seen hanging out with a *shrimp*. I mean, no offense."

Jamie Thompson must have been eavesdropping from the next table, because she giggled. I turned and gave her the Look of Death.

"I'm not offended," I told Nate. "And I know what you mean."

"Why?" he asked. "Is your dad in the army, too?"

"He was," I said, emphasizing the *was* part.

That was usually a pretty big conversation-killer, but

I guess kids who have grown up around the military are a little more used to it than everyone else. He said, "I'm sorry, man," then asked for the glue. I picked it up with extreme caution and passed it over.

When I had emptied out everything else from my folder, I saw that Bowen had kept one item: the map of Afghanistan. My eyes burned as I grabbed a Sharpie and carefully drew a star on the spot where I knew my father had died.

I glanced up and caught Nate looking. He turned away really fast.

"It's okay," I said. "You can look. I'm going to have to write about this anyway, right?"

He nodded. "Is that where—"

I swallowed. I never talked about this, and my throat felt very dry. "Yeah. He was a firefighter on an artillery base. A mortar round came in at night, hit some gas cans, and set the barracks on fire. Almost everyone was asleep in their racks, right? So my dad kept going in and throwing guys over his shoulder, then running outside through the smoke with them. Then he would turn around and run back in. The last time, his commanding officer tried to stop him— he said they were pretty sure everybody was already out. My dad's last words were, 'Pretty sure isn't sure, sir.'"

"Wow."

"Yeah. They gave my dad a medal. I mean, they gave us a medal . . . after . . ." All of a sudden, I couldn't be in class anymore. I got up and walked out of the room, really fast. Then I headed for the bathroom to splash cold water on my face and stayed in there until my heart slowed down and my legs stopped feeling all shaky.

When I got back to the room, the bell had rung, and a whole new group of kids was in there. Mr. Kurt put his hand on my shoulder and said, "Are you all right, buddy? Your pal Nate told me he thought you'd gotten glue in your eye."

"I'm okay now," I said. I realized suddenly that I basically was. It had felt good to tell my father's story.

"Well, if that happens again, please go to the nurse, okay?"

I nodded, but I was actually thinking, *In your dreams, buddy-o-rama*. I could only imagine what The Bird could do to a kid's eyeball.

When I went to my table to get my stuff, I saw that Nate had put the map, very neatly, in my folder.

I smiled.

My biggest problem was gym. We had to wear these incredibly stupid-looking purple-and-gold uniforms that read MONTVALE PHYSICAL EDUCATION on the front and STRONG

BODIES, STRONG MINDS! on the back. Personally, I thought the back should have read YES, WE LOOK LIKE DORKS! But nobody had consulted me about the design.

Anyway, there was a ten-dollar uniform fee. I couldn't remember the last time I had held a ten-dollar bill in my hand, and if I did somehow find myself in possession of one, I certainly wasn't going to blow it on this monstrosity. However, my gym teacher, Mr. Cavallero, informed us on the first day, right after he handed me my too-large "extra small" uniform, that if we didn't pay the fee soon, we could fail gym.

Actually, *informed* is a rather gentle way of saying it. Mr. Cavallero shouted the information at us, just like he shouted everything else. It was like someone had cranked the volume knob on his voice all the way up, and then spilled some of the special glue from our English class on it so it could never be adjusted back down again. And in case his own awe-inspiring loudness didn't do the job, he also carried a bullhorn, which he growled into for extra ear-shattering effect.

Seriously, the man's voice rang from the rafters.

Every day after the first week, he read a list of names out loud before class started. For a little while, the list was pretty long, but it shortened up in a hurry, until every single day, the official start to gym class was signaled by Mr. Cavallero barking into his bullhorn: "MAVERICK FALCONER." He didn't even bother to say why he was calling out my name, but everyone in there knew.

Finally, I decided I would have to speak with him, no matter how embarrassing it was, because the name thing was worse, AND failing gym would be a nightmare and a half. So I changed really fast at the beginning of the period, and then went over to him instead of heading for my spot on the gym floor.

"FALCONER!" he shouted in my face.

"I'm right here, sir."

"Do you have ten dollars today?"

My face burning, I stared down at my feet. *I don't ever have ten dollars*, I thought. *And since today is part of ever, I am going to have to say no, I don't freaking have ten dollars.*

"Um, no, sir. But here's the thing. My mom just switched jobs, and money is kind of tight at home right now, so—"

I looked up, and saw that Mr. Cavallero was also staring down at my feet—or, more accurately, at my falling-apart footwear. With a horrified look on his face, he asked, "Do you call those things sneakers?"

"Well, actually I call them Jim and Bob. Jim's the right one, and Bob's the left—"

"You're unprepared. It's bad enough that you haven't paid your uniform fee, but now you don't even have the respect to come and talk to me with proper athletic attire on? You know what? I don't have time for this! Go see Mr. Overbye!"

"But—"

"Go!"

I looked around the room, and every single kid in the gym was staring at me. Nate looked kind of sympathetic, but nobody else did. And Bowen gave me a happy little wave, like he was saying, "Buh-bye!"

Great. Now I was *really* mad. Mad enough to shoot my mouth off without thinking about the consequences. I stomped all the way to the office and opened Mr. Overbye's door before the secretaries could stop me.

He was on the phone. In a disturbingly smooth voice I hadn't heard before, he said, "I'll call you back, honey. I think I have a situation on my hands here." Then he hung up and said to me, in a somewhat less pleasant tone, "What are you doing in my office, Maverick?"

Just then, a secretary came smashing in behind me, and whacked me on the back of the head with the edge of the door so hard that some kind of framed picture fell off the door at the same time. I grabbed at my scalp, feeling for gashes, as Mr. Overbye jumped to his feet and waved her away. She backed out, mumbling apologies—not to me, but to him, because she hadn't blocked me before I had gotten into his office.

Where did the school find these ladies? She had just smashed a kid's skull with a door, so she apologized to her boss for the inconvenience? If she had shot me, would she have begged his forgiveness for the mess on his carpet?

Probably.

Anyway, The Bee picked up his photo frame, which now featured a cracked corner. Then he eased me into the chair, and asked, "Is your head all right?"

I paused for a minute before responding, because I wasn't sure. I wasn't bleeding, but there was a kind of disturbing ringing in my—

"Because," he continued, "I can call for the nurse."

"NO!" I shouted. "I mean, I'm fine. I'm perfect. In fact, um, my head's always been a bit uneven back there. I, uh, think your secretary just fixed it. Please thank her for me. Whew!"

He rolled his eyes, then leaned forward and said, "Now. Why did you just charge in here? Which you will never, ever in your life do again, by the way."

"Mr. Cavallero sent me."

"Why did he do that? Were you fighting with Bowen Strack?"

"No."

"Were you fighting with someone else?"

"No!"

"Were you being rude, or disrespectful, or breaking the rules of the gymnasium?"

"NO!"

"Then what happened?"

"Mr. Cavallero kicked me out of class for being poor!"

My eyes burned. I swallowed. I had just done something really scary. See, grown-ups always tell you that lying is the worst thing you can do, and that might be theoretically true. But in practice, the worst thing you can do is blurt out a truth that nobody wants to hear.

The Bee sighed, took a long moment to study the framed item that had fallen from his door, and then turned it toward me. It was just a fancy piece of cream-colored paper, with a sentence written on it in black calligraphy: *Be kind, for everyone you meet is fighting a hard battle*. I realized that the sentence had been hanging behind me the other times I had visited his office.

Whenever he had looked over my head and then gotten quieter, it was because he had been reading that quote.

"Maverick," The Bee said, "you aren't the first student who's come in here complaining about Mr. Cavallero's yelling. 'He screams in my face!' they say. 'He never listens to me,' they say. It's an extremely tough situation, Mr. Falconer.

"I'm going to tell you something I've never told another student, although I have trusted a few parents with it. Mr. Cavallero is one of the gentlest men I know. Would you believe his hobbies are knitting sweaters for disabled veterans and organic gardening? But he has a problem. Back in 1972—we're talking a long time ago, before I was even *born*—Mr. Cavallero was a Marine in Vietnam. An artillery round exploded right next to him, blew out his left eardrum, and damaged his right one pretty badly. Maverick, your gym teacher yells because he can't hear very well. He doesn't even know he's doing it."

That was a sad story and all, but the guy had also been a jerk about my problem. "But—but—I told him my mom couldn't afford to pay the gym uniform fee, and then he started screaming at me about how I had disrespected him by wearing ratty sneakers to his class. I CAN'T AFFORD NEW SNEAKERS! THAT'S THE POINT! It's like he didn't even . . ."

"Hear you?"

Wow.

"Were you far away when you told him this?"

"No, I was right in front of him."

"Were you looking directly at him? It's much easier for him if he can see your facial expressions and read your lips."

Darn. I had been staring straight down at the floor. I shook my head.

"I bet Mr. Cavallero got a little snappish with you, right?"

I nodded.

"It's a funny thing, Maverick. People hate looking weak. A lot of them would rather seem tough than weak, even if it actually causes them to look mean. Something to think about, isn't it?"

I nodded again. I was doing a lot of that. Truthfully, I almost felt bad for Mr. Cavallero all of a sudden.

"Now, what sneaker size are you?"

"Excuse me?"

"What size are your sneakers?"

"Well, these are a six. But they're really tight on me. I think I'm probably at least a seven by now."

"Have you told your mother this?"

"No, but . . . umm . . . she just started a new job, and we're behind on some bills. I figured I would tell her right around Christmas. That way, she can just give me the sneakers as my present."

Mr. Overbye started to reach for his phone. If he called Aunt Cat, she would start asking me too many questions about Mom, and it would be bad. If she found out I was alone from four until midnight every day, who knew what she might do?

"Please don't say anything, Mr. Overbye. I don't mind having old sneakers. I *always* have old sneakers."

He sat there for a while, silently staring down at his quote in its damaged frame. Then he said, "I'll take care of everything. But if anybody asks, you tell them I yelled at you. Because that's what *will* happen if you ever barge in here again."

I got up to leave. The back of my skull throbbed when I stood.

"Oh, wait. There is one more thing. I'm going to email Mr. Cavallero right now to explain what happened. But please take great care to be kind to him. AND I am sure I don't need to remind you that everything we've said today is confidential, right?"

"Right!"

I forced myself not to rub my head until I was out of the office. The last thing I needed was another visit to The Bird.

* * *

When I opened my locker the next morning, I found a Nike box crammed in there. I stood around trying to look casual until everyone around me had gone back into Mrs. Sakofsky's room, and then took the box out. Inside I found a beautiful new pair of sneakers.

I literally couldn't remember the last time I had owned a new pair of sneakers.

I sat down right there in the hallway, whipped off my taped-together footwear, and slipped my feet into the Nikes. They fit perfectly, and were so cushiony I couldn't believe it. It was like wrapping my feet in clouds or something.

The bell rang, and I scrambled to shove my old sneakers into the Nike box. Then I pushed the box down deep into the hall trash can before anyone could come out of class.

I felt like I was gliding through clouds all day, until I got to gym class. When I got to my spot, Mr. Cavallero was staring at me. He gestured for me to come over, so I did. Then he put one hand on my shoulder and shouted, "I GOT MR. OVERBYE'S EMAIL ABOUT YOUR FAMILY'S MONEY PROBLEMS. DON'T WORRY ABOUT THE UNIFORM FEE! WE HAVE A SPECIAL FUND FOR CASES LIKE YOURS! YOU SHOULD HAVE JUST COME AND TALKED TO ME ABOUT IT!"

I gritted my teeth and told myself, *Be kind, for everyone you meet is fighting a hard battle.*

"AND HEY! I LIKE YOUR NEW SNEAKERS! IT WAS REALLY NICE OF MR. OVERBYE TO BUY THOSE FOR YOU!"

Wow, this guy had a special talent. He didn't even have to be mean to be mean.

When Goodness Doesn't Rub Off

Getting new sneakers made me decide to jump-start my campaign of good deeds around the school. Mom was always bringing home random boxes of stuff from her new job, and I dug through to see whether anything might be useful for the cause. All I found was one of those tree-shaped air fresheners that people hang from their car mirrors. But I wasn't going to let that stop me. The next morning, I ran from the bus into school so I would get to homeroom before everyone else, climbed up on a chair, and hung the air freshener from a little pushpin over the dry-erase board.

Unfortunately, it turned out that Mrs. Sakofsky was severely allergic to the scent of tree-shaped air fresheners.

Her neck broke out in hideous hives, and she had to run out of the room to see The Bird.

I sank lower and lower in my seat, praying that Lysol wouldn't cause too much agony when sprayed onto hives.

I wasn't going to give up, though. Later that afternoon, I noticed some older girls putting up birthday decorations on a friend's locker, so I thought it might be kind of cheerful and festive to start that tradition in our class. I happened to know that Jamie's birthday was the next day, and I figured anything that made her more cheerful would be good for everybody, so the next morning I snuck into homeroom early again. My plan was to borrow one of the dry-erase markers from their ledge under Mrs. Sakofsky's board, go out into the hall, and write a joyous message on the front of Jamie's locker while everyone was saying the Pledge of Allegiance and listening to announcements. When homeroom ended, Jamie would see the decoration, and be amazed and overjoyed.

Easy, right?

Wrong.

When I got to school, the markers weren't on the ledge. So I grabbed the first marker I saw from Mrs. Sakofsky's desk, shoved it way down in my pocket—jabbing my pinkie painfully on the pin in the back of my sheriff's star in the process, by the way—and sat down at my desk to wait for my moment.

When the pledge started, I ducked out and quickly scribbled *HAPPY BIRTHDAY, JAMIE!* on Jamie's locker. Then, when the bell rang, I sort of eased my way through the back door of the room to grab my stuff without anyone noticing I had been gone.

Jamie came to the next class period a few seconds late, and I noticed she was smiling . . . and kind of blushing, too. *Yes!* I thought. I had finally done something right! I had secretly made somebody happy. Jamie kept on smiling most of the day, and I kept basking in the warm glow of my quiet hero status.

I daydreamed my way through the beginning of Mr. Kurt's class. *Who knows what I can accomplish next?* I thought. *First, the pencil sharpeners and the litter! Now the birthdays! Tomorrow, I conquer the—*

That was when Mr. Overbye barged into the room.

"All right, sixth graders!" he bellowed. "I need you to listen up. I suppose some of you have probably noticed that it is Jamie Thompson's birthday today." His voice softened and he smiled as he turned to Jamie and said, "Happy birthday, Miss Thompson."

Jamie said, "Umm . . . thank you?"

Mr. Overbye's voice boomed again: "And apparently, one of you has noticed that students in this school traditionally decorate their classmates' lockers with birthday greetings, which is a very nice thing to do. **However**, there is something else that this person has failed to notice. **Observe!**"

The Bee held up a fat marker in one huge hand. "This," he said, "is an **erasable** marker."

He raised his other hand, which held a very similar-looking writing tool. "This," he said, "is a **permanent** marker!" He leaned forward and lowered his voice to a near whisper. "Now, sixth graders, which of these do you think is the appropriate tool to use for writing on a fellow student's locker?"

I slumped down in my seat, thinking, *Well, sure, when you say it like* that, *it all sounds obvious.*

"Now," Mr. Overbye continued, "our school's custodians are tremendously overworked and underpaid as it is, so I promised them I would find the student who unintentionally added a graffiti masterwork to the face of Miss Thompson's locker. Furthermore, I promised them that the student would put on a pair of rubber gloves, grab a sponge and some industrial-strength cleaning fluid, and restore the surface of that locker to its original, gleaming appearance. So: I will be waiting at the end of the school day. I sincerely hope that the young artist will present herself or himself to me at that time for work duty—because if I have to clean that locker myself, **I will *not* be happy with this class**. Understood?"

I was extremely busy staring at a stain on my desk, but I assumed there must have been a bunch of nodding, because The Bee left after that, and class went on. For the last two periods of the day, all anyone seemed to be thinking about was the identity of the person Nate referred to as *The Mad Marker.*

Which didn't totally make sense to me. I sort of thought it should be *The Mad Markerer.* No matter what they called this person, though, all I could think about was the awful, inescapable fact that The Mad Marker (Marker*er*, whatever) was me. And if I didn't want my whole class to suffer, I was going to have to step up and admit it.

What was Jamie going to say?

What was The Bee going to say?

What was everyone else going to say?

I realized another thing, too: I was going to miss my school bus. There's nothing like trudging several miles with a heavy backpack to cap off a pathetic, embarrassing, and generally disastrous day.

When the last bell rang, practically my whole class showed up outside of Mrs. Sakofsky's room to see The

Mad Marker unmasked. The Bee was there with his sponge, gloves, and a bucket of something that was making the entire hall smell like ammonia. People were whispering and sneaking sideways peeks at one another. I heard one of the girls say, "Obviously it's not a girl, or she would have just said something already. It's got to be a boy! How embarrassing!"

I thought, *You have no idea.*

Jamie stood there, at the edge of the group, blushing again. By this point, she wasn't smiling at all.

After three or four of the most awkward minutes of my life, The Bee said, "If you have a bus to catch, you'd better run. The Montvale Bus Company waits for no man!"

Nobody budged until Mr. Overbye growled, **"Go! NOW!"** Then most of the group backed away slowly, until it was just Jamie, a couple of her friends, The Bee . . . and me. I took a deep, shaky breath and stepped forward.

"Mr. Overbye," I said, "I did it."

"You?" Jamie asked. "Why?"

"I don't know," I said.

I looked around. Jamie's friends were sort of half puzzled and half laughing at me. The Bee looked rather amused. But Jamie looked almost . . . hurt.

I didn't know what else to do or say. I reached for the gloves. By the time Jamie and her friends were out of sight, I had completely erased the word *HAPPY*.

The whole grade whispered about the "Marker Incident" for weeks, and of course Bowen had a field day. He kept humming the happy birthday song whenever I walked by, and hiding uncapped Sharpies in my bag whenever I wasn't looking, until I couldn't stand the smell of marker ink.

And, of course, Jamie didn't talk to me again for weeks. Every once in a while, I caught her glaring at me, though. It was kind of weird.

Sometimes, a good deed feels worse than a bad one.

What School Is For

The night before school started in fourth grade, my mom told me, "I know you haven't always gotten the best grades in the past, but *this year* you're going to show them just how smart you really are!"

I was like, *Mom, that's what I've done every year. The school knows exactly how smart I really am. I get decent grades, but I never get a chance to shine. That is how smart I really am.*

I remember the first morning of that year like it just happened ten minutes ago. The teacher, Mrs. Foster, jumped right into action with a lesson about similes and metaphors. Then she told us to write an essay called "What I Did on My Summer Vacation." But there was a twist: We had to use similes and metaphors in the essay.

She stood there at the front of the room, smirking like this was the most brilliant thing ever. I sank low in my seat, because writing anything about my life outside of school was dangerous. What was I supposed to put down? *At the end of June, we got kicked out of our apartment because Mom lost her ten millionth job, so we had to pack our meager belongings in garbage bags and move across town by bus*? Or maybe *The best part of my summer was the middle of July, when my mother worked at a diner for nine days. One of the cooks thought she was pretty, so he made me hot breakfast nine days in a row! Then he got caught stealing eggs and lost his job, so that was the end of the best part of my summer.*

Come on. I knew this thing was going straight onto a bulletin board. There was *no way* I could be honest about my summer.

Mrs. Foster came over to my desk and asked, "What's wrong, Maverick? By the way, what an ... interesting ... name you have!"

I couldn't tell her the real problem, so I pretended I didn't understand the difference between a simile and a metaphor. So she said, "A simile is when you compare things using *like* or *as*. So if you said, 'The water in my hotel swimming pool was as blue as the sky,' that would be a simile. A metaphor is when you say one thing *is* something else. So if you said,

'The beach towels in the Bahamas were fluffy white clouds on my skin,' you would be using a metaphor. Get it?"

I nodded, but when she walked away, I still couldn't think of a single acceptable thing to share with the class. Because as bad as the end of June and most of July had been, August had been a nonstop nightmare. When the cook at the diner got fired, Mom cursed at the manager about it, which led to her getting the boot, too. So she went home and started drinking. And drinking. And drinking. It had never been so bad before. First, I used up all the money in her purse to walk down to the corner market and buy peanut butter and bread. When that ran out after a few days, I scrounged up all the change around our new apartment and got a bunch of nearly expired snack puddings that were ten for a dollar. I ate those until one of them made me throw up.

Nothing got my mother up off the couch until the eighth day, when she ran out of alcohol. I was in the bathroom, brushing my teeth, when I heard her shuffling around. At first, I got excited, because I thought this meant the binge was over, and she was ready to start getting dressed, looking for work, finding food, and taking care of me again. But when I came out of the bathroom, she was shoving stuff into a canvas shopping bag.

"What are you doing?" I asked.

"Going out. Back soon."

My heart sank. I had seen this before. Mom was going to sell off some of our stuff so she could buy more booze. I tried to move between her and the door, but she just stepped around me.

After she left, I frantically rushed from room to room, trying to figure out what was missing. In a tiny apartment, that didn't take very long. Soon, I was shaking all over. There was only one thing missing that I really cared about. It wasn't just any old thing: It was the most important possession we had.

That was what made me call Aunt Cat, and what caused the huge, ugly battle between my mom and my aunt.

If I wanted a great metaphor to use in Mrs. Foster's assignment, I could have written, *This summer, my mother drank up my dead father's army medal.*

Instead, I just sat there and took my first zero of the year.

That gave Bowen Strack about a month's worth of material for making fun of me. He ran around school saying things like, "*I'm* Maverick Falconer. My summer vacation was like sitting in an apartment all day with no friends and nothing to do. Oops, sorry, I messed that up. I mean, my summer vacation *was* sitting in an apartment all day with no friends and nothing to do."

So you see, schools are really good at sorting us out. By the time you get to sixth grade, everybody knows who's smart, who's athletic, who's good at music, who's good at art, who's rich, who's poor . . . and on and on. There's no hiding anything for long. If the teachers don't expose you, the kids will.

I made the big mistake of thinking Nate would be different.

After we presented our poster projects in English class, Mr. Kurt gave us our first writing assignment of the year: Each of us would write a biography of somebody at our table. He got pretty excited about this. He practically jumped on top of his desk as he told us to "Dig deep, dudes!" and "Explore the person *inside* the person!"

At first I thought, *This shouldn't be too bad. All I have to do is talk Nate through my poster again, and he can write about that.*

But then Mr. Kurt said, "We need to see what's *not* on the poster, maaannn! If you really want to get a decent grade on this, you'll probably have to meet outside of school. The best thing would be if you could visit each other at home. You get a different sense of your interview subjects in their natural environments."

That was easy for him to say. He probably wasn't deathly ashamed to be seen in his *natural environment*.

Before I could come up with an excuse, I had a date to get off the school bus at Nate's house that Friday, and stay for dinner. If I hadn't been aware yet of how different rich-kid life was, that evening clinched it. When we walked up to Nate's house, which had its own little half-circle driveway like the mansions in movies do, his mom answered the door. She wasn't wearing sweatpants or anything. She looked like she was ready to go to work in an office, or maybe go out to lunch at a fancy restaurant. She knew who I was, and invited me to come to the dining room for a snack. The Fergusons had two completely different tables for eating—one in the kitchen, and one that was ten feet away in this separate room. Plus, there were four high stools and a counter in between the two. You could basically stop and eat every few steps in their house.

It was crazy.

Then she offered me choices. She made a whole speech, while Nate rolled his eyes:

"Maverick, are you a healthy snacker or a junk food snacker? Nathan here is a junk food guy. He'll sit and eat an entire tube of potato chips single-handed if you let him— isn't that right, Nate? Anyway, if you want healthy, I stopped by the whole-foods store today and got an organic-vegetable platter, with whole-grain pita crisps. Or, if you want junk, there's ice cream, tofu ice cream, frozen yogurt, potato chips, sweet potato chips, spicy yucca spears with picante dip . . ."

It was pretty overwhelming. First of all, she had already listed more food than we had in my whole apartment. Second of all, I didn't know what half of it was.

Luckily, Nate interrupted. "We have to work. Can't you just leave us potato chips and ice cream?" I was kind of surprised, because he said it in a pretty snotty way. If my mom had gone out of her way to buy me all that food, I would have been kissing the ground.

Nate's mother didn't even finish her sentence. She just put the ice cream, the chips, and some bowls and spoons on the table, and then walked out of the room.

Nate had drawn up a series of questions for us to ask each other, so getting all of his information took almost no time at all. Nate was an only child, like me. *But his family of three lived in a house with four bedrooms, three bathrooms, and a really fancy SUV parked outside.* His favorite movie was anything with Harry Potter in it. *And he could watch whatever movie he wanted on one of the family's big-screen TVs. Or his own, personal laptop. Or his brand-new Apple phone.* I didn't have a phone. Who was I kidding? I had no technology at all. I didn't even have two cups tied together with string. If I wanted to communicate long-distance with a friend, I would basically have to light a fire and send smoke signals.

His favorite food was French. I didn't even know what French food was, so I asked him for some examples. When he told me, it was all stuff I hadn't even heard of.

His biggest annoyance was when his mom didn't do the laundry on time, so his favorite clothes were dirty. *Mine was when scary teen gangsters were smoking and drinking in front of the laundry room of our apartment complex, so I was afraid to do my laundry and had to wear dirty stuff to school.*

His favorite sport was soccer. *Uh-oh—I hadn't had the world's greatest luck with the soccer players in our class. What if he started hanging out with them?*

At that point, I asked if I could use the bathroom. He said, "Sure, use mine." His personal bathroom was bigger than my bedroom. I was pretty sure his tub was bigger than my bedroom. And everything was so nice and fresh smelling. He had three different kinds of hand soap!

I was practically paralyzed by the glory of it. Plus, how was I supposed to choose? Was I more of a squirt-out-of-the-little-mermaid guy? Or a no-nonsense, yellow-antibacterial-bar man? Or perhaps a half-seashell type?

In the end, I tried all three. I left there feeling intimidated, but very, very clean.

After the interview, we played video games on the system in his room until dinner. Of course, he destroyed me at everything, because I had zero experience with this stuff. My idea of high-end gaming technology was a checkerboard that still had all of its pieces. But I had fun anyway—or at least I did until he said, "This is boring! I'm sick of these games! I can't wait till Christmas! When we get back from the Bahamas—"

That was the moment I decided his parents couldn't drive me home.

I made up a lame excuse about how my mom didn't like me to be home alone when she was working late. I asked to use a phone, and called Aunt Cat. She said she could pick me up after dinner. It all worked out fine, at the moment. It was only later that I realized something: I had called her "Aunt Cat" and Nate had seen her when she picked me up. Now Nate knew my aunt was my aunt. What if he somehow saw her at school when she was supposedly being my mom?

And, of course, the next Monday, Nate started asking when he could come over to my house. I told him every lie I could think of: My mom had the flu. Our kitchen was being redone. I had a late dance class. (*Why the heck not?*) In the end, though, I couldn't make him fail English just so I wouldn't get humiliated, so I asked if we could just do the interview at his place again. I would bring the snacks and some show-and-tell items.

He told me not to worry about the snacks, and we arranged to meet at his house that Saturday. I had to take two city buses and then walk several blocks, and I was basically dying by the time I staggered up to his door with a gigantic cardboard box in my arms and a knapsack on my back, but at least he hadn't seen my apartment. Or interacted with my mother.

I had left her a note, but I suspected she would still be out cold when I got home. Just another fun weekend of quality time at the Falconer estate.

Nate's mom had come through again on the snack front. As we worked our way through a constant flow of chips, dips, vegetables, and juices I couldn't even describe, much less name, I answered all of Nate's basic questions. Then he asked me what I had brought.

First, I opened the backpack, took out a folder, and showed him a picture I had drawn of my father's medal. I had spent hours getting the details right from memory. I had even drawn the medal's three-colored ribbon, and the plush, velvet-lined case the medal had come in. Plus, one day in school when we had free computer time, I had typed out the commendation letter that had come with it. I knew every word by heart.

"Wow," Nate said. "But why didn't you bring the real thing?"

"Um, I can't because of my mom."

This was technically true. But boy, I wished with all my heart that I could have shown him the real thing. Everybody loves a good medal. Including me.

I paused for a moment, and considered showing him my sheriff's star, which was in my pocket, as usual. But a plastic star seemed pretty lame compared to an actual medal, so I skipped that and opened the box, which contained wood chips, a paper envelope full of seed-and-nut mix, and—of course—my own personal gaming system, Freddy. He might not have had controllers, or 3-D graphics, but he was warm and cuddly, and he always stood up on his back legs whenever he saw me. Even if I was probably going to break out in hives soon from spending a whole afternoon with him.

"Uh, what's *that*?" Nate asked.

I picked Freddy up, and held him up in the light. "This is Freddy. He's my hamster. I rescued him from the pet store. He was going to die, because—"

"Ew! What's wrong with his leg?"

"Well, that's what I'm trying to tell you. It got bitten off by the other hamsters when he was a baby. He was the smallest, weakest one, so they—"

Just then, Nate's mother walked in, saw Freddy crawling up my arm, and shrieked like she had seen a giant rat.

Then she turned around and ran out of the room screaming, "Honey, there's a GIANT RAT in Nathan's room!"

Well, that explained the shriek.

Nate turned to me and grinned fiercely. "All right, I kind of like him!"

But then Nate's dad came charging into the room, holding a tennis racket aloft in one hand and a golf ball cocked behind his head in the other. He looked like he was about to go to war against the Montvale Country Club.

"Where is it?" he snarled. "Isn't this just great? And you know there's got to be more where he came from. Rats are like ants. If you see one, it means you have a hundred. Oh, this is just what I need. First, the Grumman account is giving me problems all week, and now on my one day off, I have to deal with *this*?"

"Dad," Nate said, "there's no rat. My friend just brought his hamster over for a project we're doing. For school."

"Oh, isn't this just like your mother. She overreacts to every . . . little . . . thing!"

I was thinking, *Yeah. But she isn't the one who barged in here ready for battle.*

Then, suddenly, Mr. Ferguson turned his attention to me, and smiled. "I'm sorry about this confusion. You must be Nate's new friend from school."

"Yes, sir."

"The one he was telling me about. Bowen, is it?"

I felt like someone had just kicked me in the stomach. My insides froze, even as I struggled to keep a smile on my face.

Nate said, "Uh, no, Dad. This is my other friend, Maverick."

"Well, I guess you two should get back to work, then. It was nice meeting you . . ."

"Maverick."

"Maverick."

"It was nice meeting you, too, sir." I put Freddy back in the box. The poor little guy was scared. He was shaking, and he had peed all over my forearm.

Well, at least I knew where the good soap was.

When we had written up our reports, Mr. Kurt made a display in the hallway. He attached each person's biography to their collage, and then gave us a whole class period to walk around and "learn more about our sixth-grade buds." I had come to school late that day because the power in our apartment had blinked and my alarm clock hadn't gone off. That had made me miss the bus, which meant a three-mile walk to school. I arrived just as Mr. Kurt was giving the instructions.

A bunch of black jackets clustered around my collage right away. I heard Bowen's voice from the center of the pack. In a high, mocking tone, he said, "I'm Maverick! I'm so poor, I can't even afford a whole rodent!" All the guys in the black jackets laughed in unison, and then turned toward me on their way to the next collage.

The closest black jacket to me was being worn by Nate Ferguson.

You know what schools are really for?

They're for showing kids like me our place.

Not Your Usual Christmas Tree

It's miserable on Thanksgiving when your mom is an employee at a big-box store, because you know she is going to have to work all day. It had happened to me in fourth grade (when she had just started at ArtMart) and fifth grade (House'N'Home), and sure enough, it happened again in sixth grade. I woke up that morning all alone in our apartment, and wished for the millionth time that my mother could ever hold a steady job long enough to get some seniority. Or a raise. Or, you know, anything good at all.

There was a note on the table: *Left at three a.m., home by eight p.m. Sorry I didn't tell you in advance. Just found out! Food in freezer. Love you, Mav —Mom*

That was a double shift. At least she'd be racking up the extra pay. Maybe I might even get a Christmas present this year.

I considered calling Aunt Cat, but then she would have just gotten mad at my mom for leaving me alone and working all day on a holiday. Being bored and mildly depressed was better than starting a big flare-up between the adults.

The day stretched ahead of me, empty and endless. Even kids with friends are supposed to hang out with their families on Turkey Day, so seeing other kids would have been out of the question even if I hadn't completely failed with Nate.

Well, he had tried to talk to me after the pathetic and awkward biography thing, but I wasn't going to get slapped in the face twice. If he wanted to be one of Bowen's MU clones, then he could just go ahead. It was a free country.

So I'd sat all by myself at lunch, while he got to hang out with his entire soccer team. Boy, I really knew how to punish a kid.

Anyway, I toasted a frozen English muffin for breakfast, and then sat down to watch the New York Thanksgiving parade. Which is only THE most boring and pointless thing in the world. I mean, why would I, an eleven-year-old living in the middle of nowhere, care about seeing a bunch of giant-size cartoon characters float through the streets of a big, fancy city I would probably never get to visit, with occasional interruptions for musical performances from Broadway shows I would also never see?

It was nearly as irrelevant to my daily life as school.

Just when I was so bored of the parade that I felt like my brain might explode, the horrible, half-broken door buzzer went off. It sounded like a dying goat: *BA-a . . . a . . . ah. BA-a . . . a . . . ah.*

I jumped up and rushed to answer it before whoever was there had a chance to push it again. Mom was always telling me to look through the little peephole and see who was there before I opened the door, but I was too short to do that without pulling a chair over, and then it was embarrassing when I did open the door and the guest saw the evidence of my insanely ridiculous shortness.

Which I know didn't make sense, because of course they could just look at me and *see* my insanely ridiculous shortness. But whatever.

Imagine my surprise when I opened the door and found myself face-to-face with Johnny. He was wearing a big, puffy down jacket. Next to him was a box that was nearly as tall as he was. Something spiky and silvery was sticking out of the top.

"Hey," he said. "Is your mom home?"

It was pretty cold there in the doorway, but I felt myself starting to sweat. What was he doing here? I hadn't seen him since the night he'd hit my mother, and I hadn't exactly been praying for a reunion.

"Um, no, she's not home. She's working."

"Whaddya mean, she's working? She told me she'd be here. I brought over a tree. It, uh, fell off a truck." He winked at me.

Two thoughts flashed through my mind. The first was, *Okay, it's the twenty-first century. Who still winks?* The second was, *Oh, my God. He just said the tree fell off a truck. My mom said our TV fell off a truck. Does that mean the coolest object in our house came from Johnny? Yuck!*

I must have stood and stared like an idiot for just a little bit too long, because Johnny said, "Well?"

"Oh, sorry," I said, while thinking, *Why am I sorry? Why am I always polite to people, no matter how much I hate them? Why don't I just go ahead and offer him some tea and cakes while I'm at it?* "I woke up and found a note. She must have gotten a text last night after I went to sleep. She's supposed to work a double shift."

"Well, can I come in and leave this here?"

I wasn't really sure what the etiquette was for this

97

unusual social situation. I mean, where do you direct a question like this? *Hey, my mother's abusive ex-boyfriend just brought over a tacky fake Christmas tree. Do I let him in? Should I offer him a beer? Am I supposed to hang out and watch football with him for six hours until Mom gets here?*

In the end, I just stepped aside.

After Johnny set the box in the living room, right between the couch and the TV, he left without saying another word. Then I spent several hours getting really, really mad. I mean, on the one hand, bringing someone a Christmas tree is theoretically a nice gesture. But . . .

There were a whole lot of "buts":

—But he hadn't even said hello to me. Or good-bye. Or "Sorry I busted up your mom's face."

—But he had put the tree right between my seat and the parade. What kind of jerk move was *that*? I mean, I hated the parade, but he didn't know that. For all he knew, I had been waiting all year to watch the cast of the newest Disney show lip-synch their hearts out.

—But my mom hadn't said anything about him for two months. What was he doing back in our lives at all?

—But when I opened the box to move it, I saw that the tree was a butt-ugly monstrosity. I assumed it had been stolen from somewhere. Were we supposed to be grateful to him for bringing us the lovely gift of this illegal, all-silver, spray-painted, fake-branches-sticking-out-at-all-angles, metallic horror?

—But why was I the only kid in the world whose mom couldn't find a guy smart enough to know that trees are supposed to be *green*? Geez.

I dragged the box to the corner of the room, went back to the couch, eventually found a football game, and tried to concentrate on the lovely violence. But I was too mad for even violence to calm me down. Even after watching an entire game, and half of another, I was still ticked off. It was terrible.

It got so bad that I contemplated grabbing the whole box, chucking it in the Dumpster behind our building, and not mentioning Johnny's visit at all, but I figured he had probably texted her about it. Besides, I knew my mom, and I knew that then she would feel so terrible for lying to me that she would go out and spend money we didn't have on a nice, real tree. And a nice tree stand. And ornaments, and tinsel. By the time she was done feeling guilty, we would be out of spending money for a month.

The last time she had gotten back together with an abusive boyfriend behind my back, she had blown a bunch of cash taking me to an amusement park, and then our electricity had gotten turned off.

So instead of doing what I desperately wanted to do, I decided to surprise my mom by unpacking the tree and setting it up as a surprise for her. Am I a tough guy or what?

It didn't take long, because the whole tree basically snapped together in, like, three steps. All I had to do was follow the handy diagrams that were included at the bottom of the box. Well, it was either that or learn to read the instructions, which appeared to be written in Chinese. I decided the pictures would be more practical.

When I was finished, our so-called tree looked more like the mutant offspring of a broken space-age lamp and a millipede, but unfortunately, I was pretty sure I had put it together correctly. I washed my hands, and then played with Freddy for a while—I didn't want to get any toxic metal dust from the "tree" on his fur. Usually, holding Freddy made me feel better (well, aside from the itching and sneezing), but I was so sad that even he couldn't cheer me up. Plus, he kept pushing himself into my chest like he was trying to dig a nest in my body. I think he was freaked-out by the tree.

Smart rodent, right?

After a while, I realized it was getting close to eight o'clock, so I decided to make my mom's long day easier by setting the table and microwaving two TV dinners for us. We didn't have two turkey ones, but there was a turkey one and a chicken one, which I thought was sort of close. I had just finished up when I heard Mom's key in the door.

"Hi," I said. "Dinner's ready!"

"Thanks, honey," she said, dragging herself into the kitchen. She looked exhausted. I mean, she basically always looked that way, but after a double shift on a holiday, she looked sort of yellow under the artificial lighting, and much older than usual. My day had been mostly boring, with a bunch of frustration and some anger and fear thrown in. But until I took a look at my mother, I hadn't really stopped to think about what hers had been like. She looked defeated. I hated it.

We spoke at the same time.

"Sweetie, I'm sorry about Joh—" she began.

"Apple juice?" I asked, shoving a glass into her hand.

Some people might think I was avoiding confrontation.

Others might choose to believe I simply place a high value on post-work hydration. You can be the judge.

I kept my mom eating and drinking for a while, but it was pretty inevitable that she would eventually have to say something about Johnny. I mean, it would have been kind of hard to ignore the big old glittering insectoid object in the corner, plus obviously I had been right and they had been in touch with each other during the day. Right after dinner, I cleared away the trash and glasses from the table, then fled to the couch, where I flipped channels until I found the first Christmas specials of the season.

But my mom followed, right after she poured herself a drink that was *not* apple juice. It was strangely perfect: just as the TV's speakers started blaring, "You're a mean one, Mr. Grinch!" she asked, "So, now can we talk about Johnny?"

"What do you want to talk about? I don't want to fight with you on Thanksgiving, especially after you worked hard all day."

"Oh, Mav, I'm sorry. I should have told you I was seeing him again. He started calling me a few weeks ago, and I put him off and put him off. But he's been really sweet. I honestly think he's changed."

I didn't mean to, but I must have accidentally let out a bit of a snorting noise.

"No, I'm serious, Maverick. He's been attentive and courteous, and he brought this lovely tree . . ."

I raised an eyebrow.

"I mean, it's not your usual Christmas tree . . ."

I raised my eyebrow farther.

"All right," she said, "it's a pretty awful tree. But don't you think it was thoughtful of him to bring it here and put it together for us?"

I snorted again.

"What?"

"Nothing," I said.

"What, Maverick? I'm not a mind reader."

Clearly, I thought. "Mom, he didn't put the tree together. I did. All he did was come here, put it right between me and the TV, and leave. He wasn't even polite to me."

"I'm sorry about that. Thank you very much for putting the tree together. And for making dinner. You're really something. But I think you should give Johnny a second chance. Can you do that for me?"

"Mom," I said, trying my hardest to keep my voice from breaking. "Please. He hit you!"

"But I see some good in him, Mav. I hope one day you will understand. People are very complicated, and there's good in everybody."

"Well, I think you're wrong, Mom, and I'm afraid he's going to hurt you again. But I meant it when I said I don't want to fight on Thanksgiving. Thank you for working all day to support me. I love you."

Then I stormed off to bed very, very lamely, before the Grinch's heart even had a chance to grow three sizes. Mine was feeling pretty small, too. I lay there in the dark for a long time, trying to count the number of times Mom got up, walked to the kitchen, and clinked ice cubes into her glass.

I lost track at four.

The Worst Kid in Day Care

When I was little, I used to come home every day and tell my mom about this kid who always got in trouble in my day care class. It was never anybody else, just this kid with a funny name getting scolded by the teachers again and again. We'd be getting in line for snack time, and I'd hear, "Toggler, we keep our hands to ourselves in the snack line!" Or at lunchtime, I'd hear, "Toggler! That is *not* how we drink our milk!" During outdoor recess, it was, "Toggler, we wait our turn for the slide! We do not push our friends! We do not throw mulch—EVER!"

Throwing mulch was a big problem in day care.

Anyway, the situation really troubled me. I couldn't figure out who this child was. So I thought, *How bad can he be if I can't even pick him out of the crowd? I mean, there are only, like, six boys in the group, and I haven't noticed one of them being particularly deranged. Plus, if they can yell at this kid 24-7 now, who's going to stop them from switching targets and starting in on me next?*

It was enough to turn any three-year-old into a nervous wreck. It's amazing I didn't take up smoking or something.

The problem didn't stop until one day at dinner, when my mom smacked her forehead and said, "Toddlers!"

I was like, *Say whu-ut?*

She explained, "Your teachers aren't yelling at a kid named *Toggler*, Maverick, honey. They're saying *toddlers*. That just means *kids*. They're talking to all of you at once. It's like they're saying, 'Hey, guys, we don't throw mulch!'"

I still wasn't quite sure how I felt about the whole affair, but whatever. My point is that I've never liked it when one kid gets singled out and picked on—even when it turned out to be an imaginary kid. But all of a sudden, right after Thanksgiving, a real kid suddenly became the goat of the soccer team.

Naturally, it had to be Nate. It went on all morning on our first day back, but really came to a head at lunch.

I didn't mean to eavesdrop or anything, but when you're sitting by yourself at lunch next to a group of people who are all yelling about one thing, it's pretty hard not to catch the main idea.

I was just sitting there, using the little plastic scraper device to get out the last bit of cheese from the bottom of a pack of cheese and crackers, when the whole thing erupted around me. As Nate came to the table, Bowen growled, "Oh, look, it's Mr. I-Got-Beat-By-The-Slowest-Kid-On-The-Other-Team."

I was like, *Wow, that name's never going to fit on the back of his jersey.*

Nate didn't say anything back, but Bowen never really noticed stuff like that. "Didn't you hear me, Nate? I was talking to you."

"Yes," Nate mumbled. "I heard."

"Then why didn't you answer me?"

"Well, you didn't ask me anything."

I had to admit, he had a point. But Bowen didn't seem to feel the same way.

"Oh, so now this is funny? You let that kid through, he scores, and then I have to drive home an hour and a half with my father yelling at me like a maniac about how it's somehow *my* fault. I mean, what was I supposed to do about it?"

"Well, you could have made the save," Nate said.

The whole team went, "*Ooh . . .*"

"I could have WHAT?" Bowen thundered. Heads turned. Somehow, the teachers who were supposed to be on lunch duty remained completely oblivious, but the kids were certainly tuned in now.

"You could have made the save. You know—caught the ball, deflected it, kicked it away? Isn't that what keepers are supposed to do?"

Bowen was turning an alarming shade of deep red. "So now it's *my* fault? After all I've done for you, you're blaming me because you got burned by a kid who could barely *jog* across the field?"

Nate laughed. He actually laughed. Not in a mean way, but in a "This is ridiculous" way. "Bowen," he said, "I'm not blaming you for anything. *You're* blaming *me*. I'm just pointing out that goalies make saves, not excuses. And you didn't do anything for me. I noticed your jacket two months ago and asked you about your team. You told me about it, I tried out, and I made the cut. That doesn't exactly make you my hero."

Holy cow. Nate was treating Bowen like he'd treated his mother. I wasn't sure this was going to end with Bowen offering him ice cream and then scurrying away, though.

Bowen's minions were murmuring helpful things like, "Are you going to take that, Bowen?"; "Oh, dang!"; and

108

"Wow, he really told you!" Meanwhile, Bowen's facial coloration was progressing from crimson through the various shades of violet.

I was wondering whether I should cover up the last of my lunch to avoid getting blood and teeth sprayed into my food, but the bell rang before actual violence broke out. The whole team clustered together around Nate and Bowen and headed for the hallway as one big, bloblike unit. I figured the battle would happen as soon as they cleared the cafeteria.

I didn't know what to do. On the one hand, Nate had betrayed me by joining the soccer team and laughing at me with them. Besides, he was kind of snotty sometimes, like with his mom, and he was definitely spoiled. On the other hand, if he was fighting my enemy, didn't that put us on the same side?

Also, I had vowed the night before school started to stand up for anybody smaller than me, and Nate was the only kid around who even came close to fitting that description. So far, my record in the hero department hadn't been very impressive. In three months, what had I accomplished? I had tried to save Nate, and ended up banging his head against a wall of lockers. Oh, and I had attempted to drive my mom's evil boyfriend away, but ended up constructing his hideous mutant Christmas tree instead.

That settled it. I had to take decisive action before it was too late. I packed up my lunch bag and ran out of there to catch up to the back of my class. I didn't have to run far. They were all clustered in a short, dim corridor around the corner from the cafeteria, where the teachers almost never went. The kids had formed a ring around Bowen and Nate. Bowen had grabbed Nate's shirt, and was winding up to punch him in the face.

This was my moment. I had to make it dramatic.

"UNHAND HIM, FOUL . . . UMM . . . CHEESE TOOL!"

The circle opened up to clear a path between me and Bowen, who looked puzzled. "Cheese stool?" he asked. "What the heck is a cheese stool?"

"I said *cheese tool*. With a *t*. Not *stool*, with an *s*. Cheese tool!"

"Okay, well, what the heck is a cheese tool, then?"

That was a fair question. The phrase had just popped into my head.

Nate spoke up. "Wow, Bowen, you don't even know what a cheese tool is? You're dumber than I thought."

I was thinking, *Shut up. Shut up. This is so not helping!* But Nate didn't get my telepathic message.

"A cheese tool," Nate said, as though he were lecturing our class on vocabulary terms, "is the little plastic rectangle that comes in a packet of cheese and crackers. You know, the thing you use to spread the orange cheese product. Right, Maverick?"

Everyone turned and stared at me again, including Bowen. Well, at least he couldn't kill Nate if he was focused on me.

"That's right," I told him. "That *is* what a cheese tool is. And, uh, Bowen, you *are* one!"

Bowen said, "And how is that an insult, exactly?"

"What do you mean, how is it an insult? I just called you a cheese tool!"

"Yeah, but everyone loves that orange cheese product, right? It's delicious. I would be *proud* to spread that cheese product onto crackers. Thus, you are, like, the worst insulter ever."

The crowd didn't know what to make of this. Half of the kids seemed to be muttering things like, " 'Cheese tool'? What a moron!" But the other half were like, "Dang! Bowen got called a cheese tool!"

Well, maybe one or two kids were saying, "Oh, man. I wish I had some of that delightful orange cheese product right now!"

The important thing was that nobody was beating anybody up. Until Nate said, "So, Bowen, are you going to hit me or not? You . . . cheese tool!"

It was on.

I stepped forward, trying to come up with a superhero move that would disable Bowen before he could massacre Nate. My odds of success appeared slim.

But just then, I felt a mighty hand grasp the back of my neck and propel me forward as a scornful voice spoke in my ear. "Personally, I think all three of you are a bunch of cheese tools. Nice insult, by the way." I turned and caught a glimpse of my assailant's neck. I was in the iron grip of Jamie Thompson.

"Thank you," I squeaked as she shoved me, hard, into Bowen and Nate.

"You're going to get our whole class in trouble. Did you ever stop and think of that?"

I shook my head. I was pretty sure Bowen and Nate must have shaken their heads, too. However, of course Bowen also had to say something.

"But—"

Jamie cut him off. "But what? What do you think is going to happen in about two minutes when the late bell rings and none of us are in class? Somebody's going to call

The Bee, and then we're all going to get in trouble, just because you three boneheads couldn't control yourselves."

"Boneheads?" a deep voice asked. "I thought they were cheese tools."

Either Jamie's time-estimation skills were off, or The Bee was running ahead of schedule.

Out Behind the Cheese Tool Shed

If you wanted an illustration for the concept of *socially awkward moment*, a snapshot of Nate, Bowen, Jamie, and me sitting in a row outside Mr. Overbye's office would be a pretty good one. Everybody was mad at everybody else, the secretary was giving us all the Evil Eye, and I assumed the other three were as terrified as I was about getting called in to face The Bee, so things were pretty tense in our little lineup.

"This is all your fault, Nate," Bowen hissed.

"My fault? How is it my fault? I was just sitting down, trying to eat a nice ham sandwich on rye, when you started in about Sunday's game. This is your fault, Bowen!"

"You are such a cheese tool!" Bowen replied.

"Aha!" I chimed in. "Now you're saying it!"

"Shut up, Maverick!" the other three said to me in perfect unison. Darn.

"Anyway," Bowen continued, "it's your fault because you got burned by that kid, and then my dad got mad at me. And then when I tried to point out to you how much you SUCK—"

"Language!" barked the secretary.

"Sorry, ma'am! I mean, how much you *stink*. You tried to make me look bad in front of my team!"

"Well, what do you think *you* were doing to *me*?"

"Yeah!" I shouted.

"Quiet!" the secretary growled.

"Shut up, Maverick," everyone else said.

"And then there's Jamie," Bowen went on. "We wouldn't even be here if she hadn't started shouting about The Bee. Everybody knows he has, like, super radar powers. You don't go yelling his name in the hallway. It's like saying 'Voldemort'!"

"Shh!" I hissed. "We do not speak his name!"

Everyone looked at me like I was an idiot. I thought it had been an amusing bit of Harry Potter humor, but this was a tough crowd.

Jamie's eyes flashed. "This is not my fault. I was trying to stop you all from getting in trouble. And the class. Well, *mostly* the class. I mean, I wouldn't waste my time and energy looking out for you, Bowen. And I barely know you, Nate."

She looked right through me like I wasn't even there.

"And what about me?" I couldn't help asking.

"Oh, I'm sorry. Did anybody else hear a voice coming from way down there?"

"Oh, very funny. You've only been using that joke since the third grade."

"Well, if you had grown since the third grade, maybe I'd have to come up with something new!"

Ouch. I almost snapped back at her, but then I told myself what Aunt Cat had been telling me since third grade whenever I mentioned Jamie's constant sniping: *Don't say anything—she's just insecure. Don't say anything—she's just insecure. Don't say anything—she's just insecure. Don't—*

"I'm *WHAT*?" Jamie screeched.

"BAZINGA!" Bowen yelled.

"QUIET!" the secretary shouted.

"Did I say that out loud?" I asked.

"Why would I be insecure about *you*?" Jamie asked, scorn dripping from every word. "You massive cheese tool. No, you're not even a cheese tool. You're a cheese tool kit. A complete cheese tool box. You've got, like, the little

116

scooping stick, the toasting supplies, the little wire-blade thing for slicing cheese off of big blocks, the . . . umm . . ."

"The cracker assortment?" Bowen added helpfully. Nate giggled.

Personally, I felt these people were taking the metaphor too far. But I didn't have a chance to voice my opinion, because just then, The Bee called all four of us into his office. First, he yelled at us for a while about how his job was to maintain **ORDER** in the school, blah blah blah, and how we had created an **UNSAFE ENVIRONMENT** in the hallway, **yadda yadda yadda**. Then his voice gradually built in volume and his face got redder and redder as he threw in some stuff about respecting our peers, our school, and ourselves. Just when I thought the man's head would burst like an overripe tomato, he looked past our heads, breathed deeply a few times, and calmed himself down, before saying, "Now. Can somebody please tell me exactly what happened?"

Then he sat back and smiled as we all spoke at once.

"Nothing," I said.

"Nothing," Nate said.

"Nothing," Bowen said.

"Bowen did it!" Jamie exclaimed.

Oh, sure, I thought. *She blows everything, but somehow I'm the cheese tool.*

Our only chance had been unity. Now that Jamie had cracked, we were doomed. Mr. Overbye sent me, Bowen, and Nate to three separate back rooms so we couldn't "coordinate our stories"—which I had to admit was pretty slick of him—and kept Jamie for ten minutes or so. Then he called each of us back in one by one. I was last. When Nate walked by me, his face looked completely neutral, like he was coming back from a perfectly normal trip to the restroom. When Bowen came out of The Bee's office, though, I couldn't believe my eyes. Tears were rolling down his face. He caught me looking and muttered, "Shut up!"

Then I went in and told The Bee everything. I figured I might as well, because clearly, everybody else already had. When I finished, he just sat back, folded his hands over his belly, chuckled, and said, "I like the cheese tool part. That was a nice touch. But what are you doing, Maverick—trying out to be Superman?"

I was like, *Wrong hero, dude.*

My punishment was detention, plus a call to the woman The Bee thought was my mother. Nobody else got in any trouble, apparently, except for Bowen, who got detention, too. After school, we had to sit in a smelly little mini-classroom next to the gym with Mr. Cavallero and write *I will not cause a commotion in the hallway* a hundred times.

The whole time, I just kept thinking, *I didn't cause a freaking commotion. I was trying to save my classmate from getting pummeled. Even though I don't particularly like him. And then I got ambushed, grabbed, and slammed into another kid. That's why I'm here. I should be writing,* "I will not try to protect anybody from anything. I will also not allow myself to get strangled or pushed from behind."

Bowen didn't say a word to me the entire time. He didn't even look up. When the timer on Mr. Cavallero's desk went off, he walked straight out in a hurry. This was unusual behavior for Bowen, because generally, he wouldn't have missed a chance to taunt, threaten, or otherwise torment me in a one-on-one situation. I decided to hang back and follow him at a distance.

Bowen's dad was waiting for him in a fancy sports car with the windows rolled down right outside the front door of the school. I watched from just inside the door, which was propped open a crack, as Bowen got into the car. I heard him say, "Dad, I can explain."

This should be interesting, I thought. And I was right . . . but not in any way I could have expected. Before Bowen could say another word, his head rocketed sideways toward me and I heard him whimper. It was so fast and so sudden that it took me a second to understand what must have happened.

Bowen's father had hit him, really hard, on the side of the head.

Then Mr. Strack started yelling. And I am not talking about a quiet scolding or a harsh tone of voice. I mean he was yelling like Mr. Overbye at the very top of his range, without any of the quiet parts.

The very first thing he said was, "Bowen Gregory Strack, you are an embarrassment." Then things got bad. After a minute or so, I felt guilty even hearing, so I kicked the doorstop out and let the door swing shut. I could still see Bowen's dad's insanely enraged face, though, and Bowen's look of horror. It was awful.

Right in the middle of the whole thing, Aunt Cat pulled up right behind the Stracks in her little VW. I didn't know what to do, because I didn't want Bowen to know I had seen any of this, but then Aunt Cat started honking her horn, and Bowen looked around. He caught a glimpse of me through the window set into the school's door, which left me with no choice.

I walked out and tried hard to pretend I hadn't seen anything unusual. Bowen's father had stopped shouting, at least. I glanced at Bowen as I walked past, and he just stared at me miserably.

When I got into Aunt Cat's car, she said, "Mav, just so you know, I can't keep leaving work unless it's an emergency, okay? I could lose my job if I do this too often." I nodded. Then when I tried to fasten my seat belt, she must have seen that my hands were shaking. She asked me what was wrong, and I told her everything that had happened that day. At the end, she said, "We have to talk about your, um, heroic tendencies, buddy. This is the second time this year you've gotten in trouble for the exact same thing. When are you going to learn?"

"Learn what?"

She sighed. "So it's going to be a while, then?"

She insisted on coming into the apartment, which I didn't like. What if Mom had left it a mess? What if there were bottles of booze all over the place? What if it reeked of cigarettes and last night's garbage? Aunt Cat was already in a lecturing mood. I didn't want to hear her thoughts on our unique housekeeping style.

I tried going in ahead of her, but as soon as I had turned my key in the lock, Aunt Cat edged her way past me and turned on the lights.

"Oh, Mav," she said softly. "Why didn't you tell me?"

I peeked around my aunt and sucked in some air through

my teeth. The place looked like it had been attacked by Vikings. To our left, in the kitchen, the sink was overflowing with dirty dishes. The trash can had tipped over, and some kind of leftover food had spilled onto the floor. On the table, the ashtray held so many cigarette butts that I knew my mom hadn't been the only person in the apartment since I'd left for school. Judging from the general state of things, it looked like she'd invited over a biker gang. An unhappy biker gang.

The living room was worse. The level of mess was about the same, but there, tilted sideways on the couch, holding a bloody towel under her nose, was my mother.

"Honey," she said, "you're home early!"

"Umm," I said, feeling like I was going to vomit, "actually, I'm home late. What happened here, Mom? Are you okay? How come you aren't at the store?"

She waved her hand vaguely, as though she were shooing away a fly. "The store appears to have 'terminated my probationary employment due to excessive lateness.' Can you believe that?"

Oh, I could.

"Again, Mom?" My voice sounded whiny. I hated when my voice sounded whiny.

She didn't respond to me, but looked at Aunt Cat instead. "Catherine! How lovely to see you! Pull up a . . . well, we don't have any chairs in here anymore. But make yourself comfortable. To what do we owe the honor of your visit?"

Aunt Cat strode over and knelt in the filth in front of my mom. "What happened to your face, Jessica?"

Mom looked down at the towel in her hand, and almost seemed surprised to see it there. Maybe she was. I could smell the alcohol rolling off her from across the room.

"I dunno," she said. "I had some friends over and things got sort of crazy in here. I hit it on the edge of the doorway, I think. Doesn't matter. It's not bleeding anymore. In fact, I was just about to take a nap. You don't mind if I just close my eyes for a minute and . . ."

Just like that, she slumped over and passed out. Aunt Cat pulled me into my bedroom.

"Maverick, you can't stay here tonight," she said.

"I have to. I have to take care of Freddy. And my mom needs me," I said.

"Your mom needs help. But it doesn't have to come from you. How long has this been going on?"

I looked away.

"Maverick."

"Umm . . . I don't know. She's not always like this. She hasn't had one of these bad days since the night before school started. Mostly, she holds it together. Until . . ."

"Until she doesn't."

I nodded.

"Mav, listen. I grew up like this. So did your father. I know what it does to a child. I want you to know something: If things get too rough here, you will always have a home with me. Do you understand?"

I nodded again.

"You just call, any time of the day. Or night. I know what I said about my job, but it doesn't matter—I'll get you."

I started to cry. From the other room, I could hear my mother begin to snore.

Aunt Cat looked toward the hallway, sighed, and said, "All right. Tonight—but just for tonight—I'll stay here. But I can't get sucked into taking care of your mom. I don't know what to do. She's made it very clear that she doesn't want my help, and I'm afraid nothing is really going to change for her until she decides she's ready."

Despite everything, I felt a tiny smile pulling at my lips. Aunt Cat was going to stay over!

"Now, as long as I'm here, we might as well get this place cleaned up. It's disgusting!"

We got to work. It took hours, but by the time we were through, the apartment looked—and smelled—almost like the kind of place where normal people lived. Well, normal people who really, really liked spraying bleach onto every exposed surface. That made me wonder what it would be like to live with someone like Aunt Cat. Someone who had life under control.

I fell asleep wondering that, and feeling guilty about it.

Hard Battles

For the next several days, Bowen was absent from school. I kept finding myself gazing at his empty seat in class and wondering whether he was staying home because he had visible bruises. Was I supposed to tell somebody what I had seen?

A big part of my brain kept telling me that Bowen's problems weren't mine. But another part of me was saying, *What do heroes do, Maverick?*

I kind of hated that part.

Meanwhile, I was having some very intense conversations. In English, we were learning about myths, legends, and fairy tales. Mr. Kurt paired us up and assigned us to make posters. Nate and I were supposed to illustrate some common characteristics of fairy tales. We grabbed a box of markers and a big sheet of poster board, and got to work.

I said, "How about good versus evil?"

Nate said, "How about wicked stepmothers?"

I said, "Uh, okay. And then there's magic, right?"

Nate said, "Wicked stepmothers!"

"Sure, got that. How about, um, princes and princesses?"

Nate stomped his foot and shouted, "Wicked stepmothers!"

And then it hit me. "I'm just going out on a limb here, but is your mom actually your—"

Nate literally bared his teeth at me. It was like he was suddenly turning into the world's smallest werewolf. Werecub. Whatever—he got seriously mad, seriously fast. "She—is—NOT—MY—MOM!"

Mr. Kurt started walking toward us. "Buds, is there something going on here that I should know about? Because coloring is supposed to be a mellow exercise. Don't ruin the vibes, man."

"We're fine," I told him, smiling weakly. "Nate is just a very passionate colorer. Nate, you can have the red marker. I'll take the purple one. It's all good now." Then I turned back at Nate and whispered, "So that's why you were so rude to her when I was there."

"I wasn't rude to her. I just wasn't nice to her. She's the evil snake woman who replaced my mother. What am I supposed to do, pick daisies for her every day?"

"Whatever. Just forget I said anything. Now, how about lessons? Fairy tales always have those, right? What should we put for—"

"Here's a lesson: I did *not* need your stupid help with Bowen. I didn't need it at the beginning of the year, and I didn't need it last week. I will never need your help. Got it?"

"Dude. What is your problem? I was just trying to be nice. Bowen picks on me, too, so I thought it would be nice if I helped you. Don't worry. I won't do it again."

"See, there's your problem, Maverick. You haven't learned the only lesson that even matters."

"Oh, yeah? What's that? Be mean to everybody?"

"No. *Don't try.*"

That was when something else dawned on me. "Bowen was right. You should have stopped that goal, right? You blew it on purpose."

Nate didn't say anything.

"Why would you do that? If you're good enough to be on the stupid United team, why would you just blow it?"

"Because my stepmother works with a mom from the other team. And before the game she bragged about me to this lady. It was incredibly embarrassing. She was like, 'Wait till you see my Nathan play. He's the best defender we have. Nobody gets by him!' I just wanted to die!"

I couldn't believe Nate was complaining because he had a parental figure who took an interest in his life, came to all his events, and even bragged about him. That seemed like a pretty great deal to me. I mean, I didn't even *have* events, which meant that the rest of Nate's situation was like some kind of unimaginable dream world to me.

"Yeah, it sounds like she really hates you. I can see how rough your life is."

"She doesn't hate me. She thinks I'm some kind of trophy. I'm supposed to be part of the perfect life that came with my dad."

"So you purposely mess up your life just to annoy her?"

"Pretty much."

"Wow, that's genius."

He completely ignored my sarcasm, and said, "*I* think so."

"I still don't get it, though. Why did you even bother to join the team, then? I mean, you were so excited to hang out with those guys that you freaking dumped me overnight when you made it."

"Uh, well . . . sorry about that. But I love soccer."

The period ended before I could even begin to understand that. How could a kid who loved soccer so much be willing to sabotage his own playing just to irritate his stepmom? It was like cutting off your leg in the middle of homeroom because you hated the school custodian, and you knew he'd have to clean up the mess. Nate was going to suffer a lot more than his stepmom had.

At lunch, while my head was still spinning from that little chat, a shadow fell over my pathetic, congealed school burrito. I looked up and found Jamie standing over me.

"Mind if I sit?" she asked.

Mind if I die of shock? I thought.

She sat. What was this about? Was she going to choke me again? Or maybe she had developed some new jokes about my height and was dying to try them on me. Perhaps she was going to slip some poison into my refried beans. If so, that wasn't going to work, because I never ate those. I mean, have you ever looked at school lunch refried beans? Ours looked like re-re-re-refried beans. And I wasn't so sure about the "beans" part. Anyway—

"Maverick, I'm sorry."

I spluttered, and small bits of burrito flew out of my mouth. Wow, she had managed to choke me without even making physical contact! She was turning into a ninja or something. Jamie, the Touchless Assassin. I had to admit, it had a nicer ring than Maverick, the Miniature Cheese Tool.

"You're *what*?" I asked as soon as I could breathe.

"I'm sorry."

"For choking me? For pushing me into Bowen? For making fun of my height? For telling Mr. Overbye everything so I ended up in detention next to my archenemy?"

"No. Yes! I mean . . . I'm not sorry I stopped the fight. But I'm sorry I got you in trouble. I was trying to protect you, not make things worse."

I felt my ears getting red. I hated when my ears got red, and somehow it only seemed to happen when Jamie was around. "What do you mean, you were trying to protect me?"

She was wearing a gold locket. She looked down and played with it between her fingers for a while, then said, "I didn't want you to fight Bowen, okay?"

"Why not?"

Now she looked up, and I couldn't decide if she was angry or embarrassed or sad. Actually, I couldn't decide whether *I* was angry or embarrassed or sad. Maybe each of us was all three at once.

"Because I didn't want him to hurt you! Have you *seen* Bowen, Maverick? He's twice your size!"

I didn't mean to, but somehow I found myself practically shouting at her. "I know! Because you've only pointed it out, like, a million and one times!"

Then she was shouting, too. "THEN WHY DO YOU KEEP PICKING FIGHTS WITH HIM?"

Everyone was staring. Or at least, I felt like they were. I was too mortified to look around.

"I don't pick fights with him, Jamie. He picks fights with me."

"He sometimes picks fights with you. But both times with Nate in the halls this year, you weren't even involved until you went charging in and attacked Bowen in front of everybody."

"Well, sure, that's *technically* true, but—"

"But nothing. I just don't want you to get your face smashed in."

I didn't know how to react to this. I tried smiling.

"Oh, shut up," she said. Then she got up and walked away, leaving me to figure out what had just happened.

I wasn't sure what was scarier: Jamie or the refried beans.

Things You Don't Say

I basically tiptoed around my mother for a few days. It was a strange time. I wasn't used to seeing her during the week at all, because she had been working the middle shift for months. Also, I was pretty sure she remembered the scene with Aunt Cat—I mean, it would have been pretty hard not to notice the miraculously clean appearance of our apartment—but she hadn't said a word about it. Plus, Mom must have been seeing Johnny, but she was making sure he was never around the apartment when I was home.

So, yeah. It was just like what we did after every other time she'd completely lost control. We pretended nothing had happened, until we couldn't anymore. Because this time, it wasn't just her and me involved.

Aunt Cat started calling every day, asking whether my mom was all right, whether there was anything I needed, and whether she should come pick me up. On the fourth day, my mom got mad, grabbed the phone out of my hand, and actually hung up on her.

Then we sat and ate leftover frozen franks in blankets from her former job in complete silence for maybe ten minutes, until suddenly someone banged on our apartment door. I answered the door, and of course it was Aunt Cat.

It was another of those *What do you do?* situations. Was I supposed to let her in? Slam the door in her face? Grab Freddy, jump in her arms, and beg her to take us away? Run out myself, and leave her and my mother to battle it out?

I probably should have gone with that option.

Instead, I let her in. As soon as my mother saw her, it was *on*. All Aunt Cat had to say was "Hi."

Then Mom unloaded. "Hi? *Hi?* Is that all you have to say to me? Who are *you* to be calling my son and checking up on me every day? I don't know what he's been telling you, but I'm fine. And besides, do you think you're suddenly Little Miss Perfect? Like I'm not the one who came and got you in the middle of the night when your boyfriend kicked you out while you were going to that fancy college of yours? Speaking of which, when was the last time you even had a boyfriend? You're practically a *nun*. But I'm supposed to sit here and take it while you're judging how I parent my child? You think it's so easy being a single mother? Why don't you try it, then?"

I wished I could sink down through the floor and disappear. I wished I could wash out my ears with special soap that would erase my mom's hateful words from my brain.

Aunt Cat's fists were clenched. So was her face, if that makes any sense. But her voice was completely flat. She sounded like a prerecorded message. In a way, that was scarier than yelling would have been.

"Jessica, you're in worse shape than I thought. Maverick hasn't been telling me anything. I guess he was trying to protect you. He's very loyal to you. He's *too* loyal to you."

Mom opened her mouth to reply, but Aunt Cat cut her off. "You need serious help. When you're ready to accept it, I promise you this: I am ready to take your son into my home and take care of him for as long as it takes. I care about him, and I care about you. Even when you're acting like this."

Then she turned on her high heels and started to leave.

My mom shouted after her, "GET OUT!" Which was pretty lame, considering Aunt Cat was already about three steps from the door.

I braced myself for a massive door slam, but Aunt Cat barely clicked the door closed behind her. Even though she must have been furious, she wasn't showing it.

Still, I would have been afraid to be the next person in her haircut chair.

I was a little bit mad at my mother, and a little bit scared to be near her, too, so I went into her bedroom and got Freddy out. Then I set up a maze for him on the living room floor using my textbooks and some toilet paper rolls from our recycling pile. I left a trail of seeds right up the middle of the maze for him to follow.

Freddy can't walk right because of his missing paw, but he learns fast, and he always seems to love following the trail from one seed to the next. When he finished the maze, I cuddled him up to my chest, and we watched Animal Planet for a while with the sound off. Sometimes the noises from the bigger animals scare him, but when the TV is muted, he seems to get pretty into it.

Mom kept pacing around the apartment, straightening up clutter, going to the kitchen for drinks of water, and moving random stuff around. Every time she passed near me, she stood over me for a while, like there was something she wanted to say. Once, she might have even cleared her throat. I didn't look away from my hamster, though, because I was sort of afraid I might cry if my mom and I started talking. Or worse, that *she* might cry.

I was almost jealous of Freddy. His life was so simple. Sure, he was missing a paw, but all he had to do was eat whatever food I put in front of him, drink from his water bottle, and hang out in my nice warm hands. And he could always trust me to keep him safe.

The next morning, Bowen reappeared in school. He seemed all right, but I wondered what he would have looked like if I had seen him the week before. It was the weirdest thing: I almost felt sorry for him.

Until he opened his mouth.

It happened at our lockers on his second day back. Jamie and I got out into the hall first, and she said to me, "Remember, you are *not* going to start anything with Bowen, right?"

"Why would I start anything?"

"Well, he's been kind of mad, because . . . umm . . . apparently, some of the guys were calling him a cheese tool at soccer practice yesterday after school. At least, that's what I heard last night."

"So you mean he's going to start something."

"Uh, yeah, I guess."

"In that case, don't worry about a thing. I'll be nice. You'll see."

"NO!" she wailed.

"What? You said to be nice, so I'll be nice."

"I didn't say to be nice. I just said not to start anything. Bowen hates when people are nice."

Because that makes sense, I thought. But I kind of knew what she meant. Bowen seemed to think that being nice was a sign of weakness. If he thought someone was being too nice, he might pounce.

"All right," I said. "I'll be moderately unfriendly, but not aggressive."

She beamed. "Perfect!"

Jamie walked into homeroom. And then Bowen was next to me, glaring.

"Uh, welcome back," I said. *Stupid*, I thought. *Too friendly*.

"Yeah, I'm sure you really missed me. Thanks for the new nickname, by the way."

"Uhh . . . you're welcome?" That probably wasn't actually the brightest response, but come on—what was I supposed to say?

"Are you being sarcastic with me?"

"No. Why?" *Crud. That sounded sarcastic.*

"Because . . . oh, never mind. Just stay out of my way."

"Okay."

He fiddled around in his locker for a while, and so did I, because I couldn't find a worksheet that was due for math class. I'm not generally known for my locker neatness. I mean, it's not like anybody gets famous for locker organization. But my locker kind of explodes when I open it. So anyway, the worksheet was somewhere in a massive ball of papers at the bottom of everything I owned. I had to move my jacket and textbooks onto the floor first, and then start going through the papers layer by layer, in order to have any chance of finding the stupid homework sheet.

I got down so deep into the bottom of my locker that I felt like I should be wearing one of those miners' helmets with a lamp attached to the front.

Then I heard Bowen's muffled voice from far above. "And whatever you thought you saw the other day in my car, you *didn't* see it."

I stopped looking for my worksheet. I stopped moving. I almost stopped *breathing*.

"Come on, Falconer," Bowen said. "Aren't you going to say something?"

I still didn't move. Then Bowen must have kicked the metal frame between his locker and mine. The noise and vibration were like being inside a gong. I jerked my head up and back, nearly tearing my left ear off against the edge of my locker door.

"Oww! What do you want me to say, Bowen? I'm sorry you started a fight, and then got in trouble with your dad for it?" I clutched my ear, which felt like it was cut pretty badly. I really hoped Bowen didn't decide to take a swing at me right at that moment, because I was afraid I might bleed to death if I had to stop pressing on the ear in order to defend myself.

I did the Mr. Overbye trick. I stared over Bowen's head and forced myself to breathe. Then I spoke as calmly as I could. "Bowen, it looked to me like your father punched you. I am sorry that happened."

Oopsie, now I had done it. I had been nice to Bowen Strack.

"My father didn't punch me. You must be blind. Or maybe you just couldn't see from way down at your low level, you stupid, shrimpy little *idiot*."

He slammed his locker, nearly breaking my right kneecap with the door, and stormed off into homeroom. Then the bell rang, and as the class filed out, Jamie saw me crouched there, bleeding onto my pile of papers. I finally found the math sheet, just in time to spatter it with a few big drops of gore.

Splendid.

Of course, as soon as I got to class, Jamie whispered something to the teacher and I got sent to the nurse. On my way to The Bird's office, I realized something weird: Bowen and my mom had reacted in the exact same way. They had both lashed out when somebody got close to the ugly truth, even though they were the ones who had brought it up in the first place.

I didn't get it.

The Bird sat me down and actually asked me, "What seems to be the problem? What symptoms are you having?"

I was like, *I keep feeling this weird urge to clasp both hands to my ear, and all my tissues have turned red. Do you think this means anything?*

But then she leaned in very close to my face, stared for a moment, and said, "Oh, dear. Don't panic, but I think you're, um, bleeding?"

She gently pulled my hands, and the tissue I'd grabbed during my one second of math class, away from the side of my head. Then she said, "Yes, you're definitely bleeding."

And you're definitely the smartest nurse in this whole building!

"All right," The Bird intoned ominously, "there's only one way I'm going to be able to stop this bleeding. But it's going to sting a bit. And I'm not really supposed to be doing this in school, so I'd appreciate it if you kept this on the—how do you kids say it nowadays? On the down deep?"

"Uh, I think the expression you're looking for is 'on the down low.'"

"Excellent. Can you keep this on the up tight?"

"The down low."

"Exactly. That's what I said. Anyway, I'm going to use an oldie but a goodie on your ear. It's called a styptic pencil, and it will stop the bleeding right away. Shrinks those blood vessels right up! The only negative is the stinging. Did I mention that part?"

"Yes, I believe it came up," I said. Meanwhile, I was thinking, *Holy cow! This is a woman who routinely sprays Lysol on open wounds. How badly must this stuff hurt if she feels the need to mention it repeatedly?*

Unfortunately, I found out.

It sure did stop the bleeding, though. And I was pretty sure my class couldn't hear my agonized yelps from two halls away.

I got through the next few classes by completely avoiding contact with Bowen. I even managed to stay out of his way all through lunch. It was Mr. Kurt's class that did me in.

When we got there, he announced that we had a special guest. It was a puppeteer. I was like, *Hey! Welcome back to kindergarten!*

Apparently, when he wasn't being an overly friendly hippie, Mr. Kurt spent his spare time befriending bizarre children's artists. Today's oddball was called The Incredible Oswaldo, and his mission in life was to teach children about fairy tales through the use of lovable handheld sock puppets.

I thought, *I guess once your parents name you The Incredible Oswaldo, it sort of does narrow your career options. But seriously, puppets?*

While The Incredible Oswaldo was getting set up for his show, which was titled—I'm not kidding—*Fairy Ridiculous Fun*, Mr. Kurt warned us that if we didn't behave, we wouldn't have any more special guests.

"*Special dorks* is more like it," Bowen stage-whispered.

Mr. Kurt gave him what, coming from Mr. Kurt, qualified as a Look of Death. From any normal teacher, it would only have been a Look of the Common Cold, or possibly a Look of Mild Bowel Discomfort. But at least it made Bowen shut up for a while.

Then the show started. I had to say, the "Incredible" part might have been a stretch, but this guy was at least worthy of being called The Perfectly Adequate Oswaldo. Or maybe The Mildly Talented, But Definitely Better Than Worksheets Oswaldo. Somewhere in that ballpark.

He did sock-puppet *Snow White and the Seven Dwarfs*. Well, *Snow White and the One Dwarf with a Lot of Different Accents*. Then there was *Rumpelstiltskin on Strings*, followed in rapid succession by *Hansel and Gretel Get Tangled Up in Oddly Non-Sibling-Like Ways*, and then an emergency intermission, during which The Now-Flustered Oswaldo asked Mr. Kurt for his sharpest pair of scissors.

I thought, *That doesn't sound good. Maybe Hansel and Gretel would have been better off with the witch.*

The second half of the show was, unfortunately, different. It involved ventriloquism. And a small dummy. And—for reasons known only to The Increasingly Eccentric Oswaldo, who left the room for a moment and came back in wearing a long blond wig—cross-dressing. It struck me that his hair was the exact same shade as Jamie's. I wasn't the only one who noticed.

I knew I was in trouble as soon as Oswaldo sat down and put his dummy on his lap. The dummy's hair was the same color as mine. I thought, *Oh, no. This is like third-grade field day all over again. Please don't notice, Bowen. Please don't notice. Please don't—*

Before The Doomed Oswaldo even had a chance to begin his skit, Bowen shouted out, "Hey, look! It's Jamie and Maverick!"

The whole class cracked up. I mean, except for Jamie and me. And maybe Nate. He was sitting right next to me, and I was pretty sure he only fake laughed. But still. After the way Bowen had abused him, why was he still even bothering to fake it? Nothing Nate did made any sense.

But I had other things to worry about.

Oswaldo seemed to be doing some kind of comedy routine about an elf and a fairy princess, but I couldn't hear any of the dialogue, because Bowen was substituting his own, just loudly enough that every kid could hear what he was saying, but Mr. Kurt didn't seem to notice. That was probably because he was messing around on his laptop.

I had to admit, Bowen had a certain flair for evil. Anyway, his lines went something like this.

JAMIE (high-pitched voice): Oh, Maverick! What did you say? The evil wizard has cast a spell on you? And now you're the smallest elf in the kingdom?

MAVERICK (even higher-pitched voice): Yes! Help me!

JAMIE: I don't know, Maverick. The last time I tried to help you, you knocked out my two front teeth. Then I went to the wizard for help, and he turned me into an ugly giant!

MAVERICK: But you can't just leave me like this. I'll be eaten by an eagle. Or a hummingbird. Or a really hungry mosquito. Maybe—

JAMIE: Maybe what?

MAVERICK: Maybe you could just kiss me. That *always* works in these stories!

JAMIE: That sounds kind of risky. You're so small. What if I accidentally swallow you?

MAVERICK: Oh, Jamie, for a kiss from you, there's no chance I wouldn't take. Now, bend down here and smack one on me, you titanically huge mega-babe.

JAMIE: Mmm . . . mmm . . . mmm . . . this is great . . . I mean, I *think* I feel something. Like a teensy little tickle.

MAVERICK: Whooooaaaa! This is like kissing a Transformer!

JAMIE: Ah . . . ah . . . ah . . . ahchoo! Oh, no! He's GONE! I just sneezed away my mini-elf boyfriend. What am I going to do?

During this entire horrifying scene, I sat slumped in my chair, too embarrassed to move or say anything. I didn't want to get in trouble. And I didn't want to get in another scene with Bowen after I'd told Jamie I wouldn't. But I wasn't sure how much of this I could take before I snapped. I decided to count down from ten and then *take heroic action*, whatever that meant.

I made it to three.

Shattering the Star

That was when Jamie jumped up out of her seat and said, "Shut up, Bowen Strack, you drooling, evil gorilla!"

His friends started to make their usual *ooh* sounds. In response, she spun around, pointed her finger at each of them in one sweeping motion, and said, "You, too! You're all too immature to *live*. I swear to God, if Bowen didn't tell you to *breathe*, you'd probably all suffocate."

The Defeated Oswaldo sadly placed his hands in his lap, and Mini-Elf Maverick collapsed in a heap. I knew how both of them felt.

Mr. Kurt asked Jamie, "What has gotten into you? My friend here is trying to put on a show for all of you. Why on earth would you suddenly jump up and ruin it?" He looked like he might cry.

This was definitely the most pathetic English class ever, and that included the time I'd glued the Captain to my finger. Plus that other time in second grade when that one girl had wet her pants at story time, and then tried to pretend a puddle of apple juice had mysteriously appeared all around her. Her family had moved out of town within a month. Coincidence? I think not.

Anyway, Jamie laughed. That was never a good sign.

"I didn't ruin your class. *Bowen* did. How did you not hear him? Every kid in here did. He was making fun of me under his breath for the last five minutes while you were checking your email."

Oswaldo gave Mr. Kurt an injured look, and Mr. Kurt shrugged at him. Then Mr. Kurt said, "Whatever you heard, young lady, I didn't notice any disturbance until you stood up and stopped the show. You will write my friend here an apology letter by tomorrow."

"But Bowen—"

"Is that understood?"

"But—"

"I said, is that understood?"

Jamie nodded.

Wow, she had gotten Mr. Kurt so mad, he had forgotten to be a hippie.

Dude.

Right after class, Jamie and Bowen almost started throwing punches in the hallway. I pushed my way up to them, grabbed Jamie's shoulder, and pulled her aside.

"Jamie," I said, "I thought you said not to pick fights with Bowen."

"Ooh," Bowen said, loudly enough for everyone around us to hear, "Looks like fairy tales *do* come true! Is little Mavvy going to stand up for his supersize *girlfriend*?"

"I told *you* not to fight with Bowen," Jamie said. "I didn't say *I* wasn't allowed to kick his butt."

"Oh, she's feisty, too! Is that how you like your women, Maverick? Big and spicy?"

Jamie turned away from me and raised a fist. I reached up, grabbed her arm, and said, "No! This is what he wants!"

"Hey! It's Maverick, the Elf Psychologist!"

Jamie said, "Come on, Maverick! I just want to hit him once."

"Kissy kissy, Jamie!"

"I mean twice!"

"Kissy kissy, tiny Mavvy!"

"Well, you can't."

"Why not?"

"Because I'm going to hit him first!"

Some random eighth-grade teacher arrived a few seconds later, but by the end of the day, it was arranged: Bowen and I would meet at a park off school property. There wasn't going to be any backing down this time. The Bee wasn't going to show up. I felt like the whole year had been leading to this point.

Actually, I felt like we'd been heading for this fight since that day we'd rolled around next to the Dumpster in third grade.

It seemed as though everybody in the entire sixth grade showed up for the fight. I got there a little bit late, actually, because I had stopped in a school bathroom for a few moments after the last bell just to be alone. Well, that, and to have a panic attack. I locked myself into the far corner bathroom stall, which had a window ledge running all along one side, and hoisted myself up onto the ledge so my feet were dangling down. Then I tried to take deep breaths.

It was bad enough that Bowen was going to pummel me. But if I fainted at his feet before the fight even started, my cowardice would become legendary. Middle school poets would sing of it for decades to come. I needed to concentrate on something that would calm me down. I rubbed my hands frantically on the fronts of my pant legs, because my palms were dripping with sweat.

That was when I felt my dad's star, and got an idea.

I slid down off the ledge, took the star out of my pocket—carefully, because if it slipped out of my hand and into the toilet, it would be tragic. I lifted up the white hoodie I was wearing, and carefully pinned the star onto the left front of my T-shirt, right over my heart. Then I pulled the sweatshirt back down.

I thought, *Calm down. Dad was a hero. You are his son. You can do this.*

Another part of me was murmuring, very quietly, *Wait! Dad DIED a hero. Why is this comforting again?*

But I tried really, really hard to ignore it as I strode manfully out of the stall, washed and dried my hands, and headed out to the park.

The crowd parted for me as though they could feel my force field of doom. There were whispers around me, and I might have detected a few snickers. For all I knew, some people might have been placing bets, although probably the odds weren't running in my favor. I headed for the mulch-covered area between the picnic pavilion and the swing sets, where Bowen stood, surrounded by a sea of black jackets. Nate was there. I caught his eye, and he looked away.

Jamie was there, too. Apparently, she had cooled off some since the scene in the hall, because she grabbed my sleeve and said, "You don't have to do this, Maverick. It's stupid. It doesn't prove anything. Everybody knows Bowen's a jerk."

I stopped and looked up at her for a minute. She was breathing hard and fast, and I realized that she was the only kid on the whole playground who looked scared for me.

Then she said, "Besides, he's three times your size. Why should you—"

But I had already pushed past her. In the end, it was always about how the little guy is just supposed to step aside and let things happen without fighting back.

Forget that. "Let's go, Bowen," I croaked. It had sounded a lot tougher in my head.

I was rather surprised to see that Bowen didn't have his usual smirk going. "Are you totally sure you want to do this, Maverick? We're off school grounds. Nobody's going to stop this once it starts."

I forced myself to laugh. "Oh, sure," I said. "You were brave enough when you were making fun of a girl today. But now that it's fighting time, you're hoping I chicken out for you? Well, it's never going to happen. So come on!"

"You come on!" he snapped.

"Unlike you," I said, "I don't start fights. I finish them!" I thought that sounded pretty cool for a guy who was practically shaking.

Then Bowen said something else I don't remember, and I said something lame back, and each of us got shoved from behind by the crowd somehow. When we banged into each other, I put up my fists, and so did he.

It was on.

I knew Bowen had a few advantages over me—namely height, strength, reach, athletic skill, speed, and crowd support. So I figured my only chance was the element of surprise. I screamed a kamikaze scream from the bottom of my lungs, and started swinging both fists as fast and as hard as I could. Bowen stepped back. I kept swinging, and Bowen kept back-stepping, until his back hit the wall of the crowd, and they pushed him toward me again. He punched me extremely hard, once.

Dead-on in the left side of the chest.

I felt a crack, and a slicing stab of pain. I stopped swinging, started to reach for my chest with one hand, and bent forward. As I did, Bowen swung his knee up, into that same spot on my chest.

The impact jerked me fully upright, and time seemed to

stop for a moment as I looked down at myself. The entire left side of my sweatshirt was already soaked through with blood.

I looked at Bowen. He looked at me. Everybody else was suddenly running away in all directions, except for one person.

Jamie.

"Bowen," she said, strangely calm, "get your phone."

As the spell broke, and Bowen sprinted over to where his book bag lay on the ground, Jamie said, "Maverick, come here and sit down on this picnic table. Can you do that?"

Apparently, I could.

"Now I'm going to take off your hoodie, okay? And your shirt, too."

This was getting weird. But I must have nodded or something, because suddenly, my arms were up in the air, and Jamie was very gently pulling my sweatshirt over my head. Then she tried to tug on my T-shirt, and I almost passed out from a new wave of pain. "Bowen," she said, "give me your phone. Mav, we need to take you to the emergency room. I'm going to call 9-1-1."

"No!" I said. "No ambulance!" I was pretty sure ambulance rides were expensive, and I didn't think my mom and I had health insurance at the moment.

"Then we have to call someone, Maverick. Who should we call? You need to tell me a number."

I looked down at my chest. It was pretty gruesome. The star had broken, and then cut a deep slice, several inches long, just below my collarbone. Half the star was still stuck into my chest by the pin. But the shirt was still pinned to the star, too, which was why it had hurt me so much when Jamie had pulled on it.

I felt woozy. The next thing I knew, I was lying on the bench on my back. Jamie just kept saying to me, "I need a number, Maverick. Come on, give me a number."

I didn't know what to do. Aunt Cat had said she could lose her job if she got another distress call from me there—and I was pretty sure this qualified. But there was no way my mom would be able to come get me, because she didn't have a car. My throat burned as I said, "I don't have anyone to call."

That was when Bowen grabbed his phone out of Jamie's hand and started dialing. "Who are you calling?" she asked.

"My dad. He's a cop," he hissed. "Now shut up!"

"But he'll kill you!" I managed to croak.

"I know! But this is my fault, and— Hello, may I please speak with Lieutenant Strack? This is his son. It's an emergency."

Stitches and Glue

It's probably more fun to get a ride through town in a police car if you aren't bleeding all over the place, but still, I vaguely remember thinking the flashing lights were kind of pretty. The officers had sat Jamie down next to me, and she talked to me all through the ride. I was having trouble concentrating on her words, but in an odd way, it was nice not to be alone.

Jamie insisted on staying with me at the hospital while the doctor and nurses pulled the pin out of my chest, and she even watched as they cleaned and stitched my wound. She claimed to be my sister. I was developing all kinds of interesting pretend relatives. Anyway, the pain stopped after the doctor gave me a couple of shots. After that, I just felt some pushing and pulling. But I kept holding Jamie's hand the whole time anyway.

When the doctor had finished, and I was all bandaged up, Jamie and I were left alone in the little curtained-off section of the emergency room for a while. The first thing I said was, "You were so calm when I was bleeding. That was awesome."

She just shrugged and said, "My little brothers are accident-prone."

Next, I thanked her for staying with me, and then I said, "Can I tell you something stupid? I've been carrying that star around with me all year. Do you want to know why?"

"Well, it's the star your dad got you, right? I think you've mentioned it in school projects before."

"Yeah, but that's not why I've had it on me every day. I've been carrying the star because the night before school started, I decided . . . well, I decided I wanted to be brave and stand up for people if they were getting picked on. So, uh, the star was supposed to . . . I don't know . . . I guess it was supposed to remind me."

Jamie looked away from me for a long time and didn't say anything.

I knew it, I thought. *I shouldn't have told her, because it's the dorkiest thing in the world. I wouldn't have said anything if not for all the blood loss. I just got goofy and—*

"That's not stupid," she said, very quietly. "Can I tell you something?"

I nodded.

"You know how I've always blamed you for the whole three-legged-race incident?"

I smiled, just a little bit. "Yeah, I guess I kind of noticed that. A bit."

"Oh, be quiet. Anyway, the whole thing was my fault. I was the one who tripped us with my stupid long legs. But I was really embarrassed about it, because Bowen and all the other boys always called me Too Tall Thompson."

"I remember that."

"Believe me, so do I. You were the only boy that didn't. You were always nice to me. But when we fell, I blamed you for being short, instead of myself for being tall. I'm sorry. I'm so sorry!"

Then Jamie Thompson, my old tormentor, started crying, and I reached out to hold *her* hand. If it hadn't already officially been the weirdest day ever, this was the clincher.

But wait, the day wasn't over. Because just then, Bowen and his father walked in.

I dropped Jamie's hand like it was made of hot coals. Whatever blood I still had in me rushed to my face. I heard rustling as Jamie sat bolt upright in her chair. Bowen's dad made Mr. Overbye seem like a teddy bear. He cleared his throat and spoke.

"Are you Maverick Falconer?"

"Yes, sir."

"Are you feeling better now that you're patched up, Maverick?"

"I think so, sir. Thank you."

He nodded and smiled, but I could tell he didn't really care whether I felt better or not. "Good, good. Now . . . I asked my son here how you got injured, and he told me his side of the story. I told him I was going to check everything out with you. Please keep in mind that this is very serious, young man."

Bowen said, "Tell him the truth, Maverick. Please." Even though I had just lost about a quart of blood, I was pretty sure Bowen's face was paler than mine at that moment.

Mr. Strack just looked at Bowen. If all fathers looked at their sons that way, it was almost enough to make me glad for a moment I didn't have a dad.

I sat up as straight as I could, looked Mr. Strack right in the eye, and said, "Bowen and I were playing a nice, friendly game of tag, when I suddenly tripped and fell. I guess my chest hit the edge of a picnic table or something. And, uh,

I was wearing a toy badge to show that I was 'it.' The badge broke and cut me.

"Lucky for me, Bowen's quick thinking saved the day. Most of the other players ran away, but Bowen stayed. He called you, and the next thing I knew, I was in a police car on the way here.

"Seriously, sir, your son is a hero."

I felt like Mr. Strack's eyes were burning two holes through mine, straight into my brain. "That's your story?"

"Um, that's what happened. Sir."

Without another word, Mr. Strack grabbed Bowen by the arm and dragged him out of the room. But I was pretty sure Bowen flashed me a little grin before he was pulled out of sight.

I couldn't remember when, but the hospital must have called my mother at some point. She managed to get a ride from a friend, and made it to the hospital pretty fast. In the meantime, Jamie got picked up by her mom. The last thing Jamie did was ask for my father's broken star.

"Why?" I asked. "What are you going to do with it?"

"Trust me," she said. "Please?"

When your former enemy, who has just sort of saved your life, asks for your broken sheriff's star, you give it to her. Am I right?

What Glue Doesn't Fix

Mom didn't say much to me in her friend's car. We were alone for a couple of minutes when we stopped at a pharmacy to pick up some prescription pain medicine, bandages, and antibiotic ointment. Mom didn't complain about the cost of any of it, but I felt really awful, because I knew the amount would just get added to her credit card debt.

But still, she didn't say a word to me until we were in our apartment. I had no idea what to expect. First, she stared at me intensely, almost like she was trying to memorize me for a quiz. It made me nervous. I couldn't recall a time she'd ever looked at me like that before.

Then, instead of talking, she just stood there as tears began to roll down her face.

I couldn't take it.

"Mom," I said, "I'm okay. It's just some cuts. From a stupid little sixth-grade fight. I'm all fixed up. You don't have to worry about me. I swear."

Mom's reaction surprised me, to say the least. She kept right on crying, but she also yelled at me. "Maverick, I DO have to worry about you! I should have been worrying about you all along, but instead you've been trying to take care of me. Your aunt Catherine even tried to tell me that, and what did I do? I threw her out of here. I'm so sorry."

Next, she grabbed me in a bear hug and spoke into my hair.

"Now we are going to sit on the couch, and you are going to tell me everything."

Everything? I had never told my mom everything. This could potentially take weeks. I had the crazy thought that we might need to send out for water and camping supplies.

"But, Mom—"

"Everything."

"But, Mom, my chest is starting to hurt. I think the shots are wearing off."

She loosened her grip, and said, "All right. First you are going to take a pain pill. And then you are going to tell me everything."

At first, it felt strange telling my mother about my problems after trying so hard to hide every issue I had from her for so long. But as the pain medicine kicked in, I started to feel sort of light-headed and sleepy, and the words came. I told her about Jamie and the way she had treated me ever since third-grade field day. I told her about Bowen and his soccer posse. I told her about Nate. I explained my adventures with The Bird and The Bee.

When she asked me why the school had never called about any of the trouble I had gotten in, I even told her I'd put Aunt Cat down as my emergency contact person.

"Why did you do that, Mavvy?" my mom asked.

"Well, for one thing, she has a car . . ."

My mom didn't reply. She just sat there and looked at me until I continued.

"And, well, she always answers the phone. I mean, she's . . . um . . . awake and stuff."

My mother's eyes filled up with tears. "You mean, you know she won't be in some kind of . . . embarrassing condition when you need her. And you're right. I haven't been reliable. I hope you know I've been trying. But I promise you I'm going to try harder from now on. I want to be somebody you can trust."

Things were starting to get sort of blurry for me by then, but I'm pretty sure there was some quiet hugging for a while.

Finally, I told her about the big fight. Which led me to explain about my father's badge and how I had carried it around all year. How it had cut into me. How it had broken.

At some point, I must have dozed off, because somehow, I found myself in my bed, and Mom was sitting on the edge, stroking my hair and saying, "Maverick. Maverick. You never needed a badge to be my hero."

I insisted on going to school the next day, even though my chest was so sore in the morning that every breath I took made me feel like someone was sawing into me with a hot, dull blade. In homeroom, Bowen gave me a look like he was going to say something to me—but he didn't. I wondered what he was thinking, and what his night had been like. Meanwhile, when I looked at Jamie, she twitched her head toward the doorway and winked at me, like, fifteen times before I realized she wanted to go and meet at our lockers.

Everyone else must have thought she was having some kind of spasm.

Anyway, out in the hall, she dug into her backpack and took out a brown paper bag.

"Close your eyes and hold out your hand," she said.

My heart started pounding, which made my stitches burn. I closed my eyes and said, "You know, this is totally dangerous. How do I know you won't beat me up and take my lunch money while I'm blind and helpless?"

"Oh, give me a break, Mav," she said. "We both know I could do that any time I wanted with your eyes wide open." I know that sounds mean, but somehow I could hear a smile in her voice. I felt her fingers around my wrist, pulling my hand up and out in front of my body. Then, with her other hand, she placed something in my palm and closed my fingers around it.

My father's star.

I opened my eyes and looked down. The star was back in one piece! I lifted it close to my face and turned it slowly in the dim fluorescent light.

"Um, it's not perfect," Jamie went on. "I used my father's modeling glue. He builds airplanes. From World War Two, mostly. I help sometimes. And they're plastic, so I thought . . . I mean, the planes are plastic and the star is plastic, right? So why not glue the star back together? But you can still see the line in bright light. And there are brush marks. And some dried glue. But my dad said you could probably get off the dried glue with a solvent if you're really careful. And he said the star will be stronger now than it was before you broke it. I mean, before Bowen broke it. So, yeah."

Maybe it was the leftover effects of the pain medication, or maybe I just went temporarily insane. I don't know. But suddenly, I threw the arm that wasn't holding my star around one side of Jamie in a bizarre half hug. There were so many reasons why this was dumb. I mean, Jamie and I *hated* each other most of the time. Plus, because of our height difference, I was basically smushing my nose into her neck. Her *chin* was resting on top of my *head*. Oh, and there was one other thing.

Somehow, without either of us noticing, the bell had rung. So the whole class was pouring into the hall just in time to watch this awkward spectacle.

Jamie and I stepped away from each other so fast that I almost dropped the star. She noticed and reached for it. That meant we were now practically holding hands, right in front of everybody. No, worse than that—*cupping* each other's hands.

"Uh," Jamie said.

"So," I replied.

"So," she said. It struck me that her entire face was red. And her neck. And her ears. I hadn't seen her blush like this since I'd decorated her locker for her birthday.

"So, yeah. Great gluing."

Great gluing? I thought. *Who says "Great gluing"? In the entire history of the human race, when has any other boy ever said that to a girl?*

Then we both backed away, slowly at first, then faster and faster, until the hallway crowd sort of swallowed Jamie up.

All the way to first period, I ran my sweaty fingers along the front and back of the star. Jamie had done a great job. I could hardly feel the crack at all. But I still knew it was there.

I sort of liked the idea that sometimes, when you fix a broken star, it ends up stronger than it was before.

That night, Mom cooked dinner. It was incredible! Okay, the dinner itself was just spaghetti with sauce from a jar, plus premade garlic bread. But it was incredible that my mother had held it together all day, assembled a set of matching ingredients, cooked everything at the same time, and then actually sat down with me to eat. The TV wasn't even on.

She was drinking water.

I felt like I was living in a dream, or like I had come home to the wrong apartment. Mom asked me about my day. She remembered the names of all the people I had mentioned

168

the night before. She laughed when I told her about Jamie and the lockers . . . but that was kind of okay.

So of course everything had to fall apart. While we were doing the dishes together—a first—our door buzzer sounded. Mom's face got the pinched-up look she gets when she's worried, and she said, "You finish up here, okay? I'll go see who that is."

But her expression had already told me, and soon the angry murmurs that cut through the sound of the running sink water confirmed it. Johnny was in the apartment.

I turned the faucet on harder so I wouldn't have to listen to my mom and Johnny arguing. That didn't work for long, because the only things standing between them and me were the refrigerator and the little bit of wall that separated the kitchen from the tiny foyer of the apartment.

My heart was pounding against the stitches again, and I could feel sweat breaking out all over my body. I didn't know what to do. If Aunt Cat had been here, she would have told me to mind my own business, that it wasn't my job to protect my mother.

But that was easy for her to say.

On the other hand, I knew I wasn't strong enough to kick Johnny out of the apartment if he didn't want to go.

Plus, every time my mom sent him away, she always let him back in eventually, so what was the point of a confrontation?

There was a stained spot on one of the plates. I scrubbed at it harder and harder with our smelly old sponge, but the stain just wouldn't come off. I tried to concentrate on the stain. *Come on*, I told myself. *Get that stain out. Nothing exists but you and the stain. Scrub the stain. Scrub the—*

"Get your freaking hands off me!" my mother shrieked.

My hands jerked up into the air, and the plate flew up and over my right shoulder. It shattered on the floor behind me.

Well, that was one way to get rid of a stain.

"Geez, Jessie! You didn't tell me your kid was here. *Now* the freak show is complete!"

I hopped down off my dish stool and stepped around the corner into the hallway.

Boy, it felt pretty crowded. My mom was maybe two steps inside the doorway, immediately in front of me. Johnny was just one step inside, and had one hand on Mom's left arm. He pointed his other hand at me and said, "Get back in the kitchen, Maverick. This doesn't concern you."

Mom said to me, "I can handle this, Mav."

But she couldn't. If she could handle Johnny, he would have been long gone.

I squirmed my way between them, and said, "Hit me, Johnny." My voice cracked, but it didn't matter. Johnny looked shocked.

"What are you talking about, kid?"

"You think you can do whatever you want to my mom and I can't stop you because I'm small, right? But if you touch either of us again, I'm calling the police. And if you hit me, it's assaulting a child. By the way, do you want to know what my . . . uh . . . best friend Bowen's dad does for a living? He's an extremely important police officer. Think about *that* for a second. In the meantime, you'll have to get through me to get to my mom."

Johnny took a step back. He actually took a step back!

Then he glared at my mother over the top of my head. "Are you sure this is what you want, Jessica? Because if I leave now, I'm gone for good. No more help with the electric bill. No more big-screen TVs. No more Christmas trees."

She said, "I'm sure. Now go." Her voice shook, but she said it.

Johnny said, "Well, if you're really gonna . . ." Then he just let the sentence trail off as he turned around and left.

As soon as our half-broken screen door rattled shut behind Johnny, Mom angled herself past me and closed the heavy metal door. "It was the ugliest Christmas tree in the world anyway," she said. Then she clicked the dead bolt into place. I couldn't believe it. I had stood up to Johnny, and my mother had backed me up.

We had won.

Mom turned back in my direction, smiled, and said, "Well, this calls for a celebration!" Five minutes later, I was sitting across the table from her with an open, warm can of soda in front of me. She was already on her second glass of something clear that was *not* water.

Sometimes you can win and lose in the same night.

The End of Heroes

The next day during third period, I got called down to the office. As soon as I saw the look on The Bee's face, I knew this wasn't going to be one of my usual visits. He was trying to smile at me. The effect was ghastly.

"Please sit down, Maverick."

I did.

"I just got a phone call, and I'm afraid I have some awful news. There's been a fire at your apartment."

Without even realizing what I was doing, I somehow leaped out of my seat so that my palms were on the edge of his desk. "My mom! My mom was sleeping in there. Is she okay? Did they get her out? I have to tell someone she was in there. We don't have a car! The parking space in front is empty! What if they don't know—"

He stood and put a hand on my shoulder. "Your mother got out of the apartment. She's in the hospital right now. She has some pretty bad burns on her hands, and some smoke inhalation. The person who called said your mother will be all right. But . . ."

"But what?" My thoughts were racing. Had my aunt been there for some reason? Was she hurt? Had one of the neighbors been injured?

"Maverick, the fire started when your mother fell asleep with a lit cigarette. Apparently, the cigarette fell from her hand and landed on a pile of wood chips. They went up right away. That woke up your mother, who reached down into the glass tank containing the chips, and—"

"FREDDY!"

"I'm so sorry, Maverick. Your mother tried—that's how she burned her hands. But she couldn't save your pet."

A moment later, Aunt Cat ran in and found me crying like a baby while Mr. Overbye patted me awkwardly on the shoulder. The Bee looked at her and said, "Wait! Aren't you in the hospital?"

"Umm . . . I'm not exactly Maverick's mother, exactly."

"You're not exactly his mother, exactly?"

"Right."

"Then who exactly *are* you?"

"I'm his aunt. His father was my older brother. Listen, can we sort this out later? I really want to get Maverick over to the hospital. I promise you can arrest me or whatever as soon as I'm done doing that."

Mr. Overbye grabbed both of my shoulders, held me at arm's length, and said, "Are you safe with this person?"

"Yes," I said. "I trust her more than anybody in the world. That's why I told you she was my muh-muh-mom. But I'm sorry I lied."

Mr. Overbye stared into my eyes for what felt like forever. I forced myself to look straight back at him without blinking, which was hard, because my eyes were burning. Finally, he said, "Go. But this isn't over."

We had almost made it out the door when Mr. Overbye said, "One last thing, Maverick: Good luck. I'll be thinking of you."

When we got to the hospital and found my mother's room, she was sleeping. It was terrible. Her hands were all wrapped up in gigantic mittens of bandage stuff, she had an oxygen mask strapped to her face, and there were tubes going into various other parts of her. There were a couple of chairs in the room, so Aunt Cat and I sat down. I was too choked up to talk for a while, but then I worked up the nerve to talk to Aunt Cat about something that had been bothering me all year.

"This is all my fault. I should have told you right from the beginning about Mom's drinking. I didn't want you to know because . . . well, you kept saying I could come and stay with you if I ever needed to. But I didn't want to ditch my mother. And I didn't want you to think less of her, and I didn't want you to think I couldn't handle my own problems. But now . . . maybe if I had told you, you could have gotten her some help or something. I messed everything up. Last night Mom got in a big fight with Johnny, and I dared him to hit me. So my mom kicked him out. And I thought everything was great for a little while. But then she said this called for a celebration. And she started drinking. And drinking. And then she stumbled into her bedroom and passed out. I checked in on her in the morning, and everything looked fine. She didn't have any cigarettes or matches near her or anything, I swear! She must have gotten up to get some, and then gone back to bed. But it's still my fault, because—"

Aunt Cat cut me off. "It's not your fault. It has never, ever been your fault. This has been going on since before—" She stopped in the middle of the sentence and clasped her hands over her mouth.

176

"Before what?"

Aunt Cat looked down and away from me.

"Come on," I said. "*Please* tell me."

"Since before you were born."

"You mean, my mom dated loser guys like this before she met my dad? But how would you even know that? You didn't know her then. And besides, after what she had with my dad, how could she go *back* to guys like Johnny?"

Aunt Cat's eyes filled with tears. "Oh, Mav. I loved your father. He was my big brother. But when he was with your mother, he *was* a guy like Johnny."

I swallowed. My ears were buzzing. I felt nauseated. Suddenly, I felt like the entire world had stopped turning. My aunt had just said something completely impossible.

"Aunt Cat, what are you talking about? Why would you even *say* that?"

She sighed, long and slow. "I know I shouldn't be telling you this. It really isn't my place. I just can't stand to see you blaming yourself for your parents' stuff, because . . . Listen. When your father and I were kids, our parents drank too much. Your father thought it was his job to be the hero, so he would always try to protect me whenever our father got out of control. He took a lot of abuse over the years that should have been mine. That's the good part of your father.

"But then when he grew up and became a husband and a dad, he started acting out the same old pattern. He married a woman who drank a lot, and they got into violent fights with each other."

By this point, I was leaning all the way forward, rocking in my seat, my hands covering my ears. This wasn't true. It couldn't be true! My father was a hero. My mother had always told me so. I had seen his medal. I carried his star.

But then I suddenly recalled something I had never been able to remember before. I remembered why I had been angry the day he had bought me the star. We had been on vacation at the beach, and I had been sitting on the front steps of our little rental house, sifting through a bucket of sand and shells. My parents had been just behind me, on the screened-in porch, and at first they were laughing. Then their voices had gotten louder and angrier. I remembered shoving my hands into the sand faster and harder as I got more and more upset. Then I heard a sharp smack and a gasp from the porch, just as I was squeezing a big shell. The shell had cracked and cut into my palm. I jumped up and ran inside, holding my palm outward to show my parents my boo-boo.

My parents had both spoken at once.

My mother had whipped a hand up to cover one side of her face and said, "Oh, honey. What happened to your hand?"

My father, red-faced, had snarled, "I thought I told you to stay outside!"

I remembered running away, crying, and my mom bringing me back and cleaning up my cut. It must have been hours later when my father offered up the badge as a makeup gift.

I looked at my aunt Cat and whispered, "Now that you said it, I remember." She put her arms around me and held me for a long time.

When we had stayed still for so long that I was starting to get hungry and sleepy at the same time, something occurred to me. "Aunt Cat, did you ever worry that you were going to grow up and be like your parents?"

She laughed, but it wasn't a particularly cheerful sound. "Sure, all the time. I used to have trouble sleeping when I was a kid because I was so afraid I would end up like them."

I thought about this for a while, and then got up the courage to say, "What if I'm like *my* dad? What if I *think* I'm a hero, but really I'm going to be a bad boyfriend? What if I'm going to be an abuser? What if I'm already like that, but I just don't know it yet?"

She snorted. "Maverick Falconer, listen to me: You are not going to be an abuser. You don't have an abusive bone in your body. You are the sweetest, bravest, most thoughtful kid I have ever met."

"But how do you *know*? Nobody looks like an abuser at first, right?"

"Well, it takes some time and some experience. But now when I meet a nice guy, I can usually tell."

I smiled for the first time all day. "So is Bill at the pet store a nice guy?"

She looked startled for a moment, then maybe a bit annoyed. Finally, she laughed, and said, "I've signed your report cards all year. I know what your grades are like. How can you suddenly be this smart? Okay, here's the deal. When I first started dating, I ran into a couple of bad guys. Then I decided I had to do something to make sure my life didn't turn into a repeat of my parents' lives, so I purposely started making different choices."

"So it's that easy? You just decide not to do dumb things, and then all of a sudden, you're not doing dumb things anymore?"

My aunt laughed. "Easy? It's hard. Sometimes making the right choices is super hard. But if I did it, I know you will, too."

"Thank you, Aunt Cat. But you never answered my question about Bill."

She smiled. "You're absolutely right. Now, do you want to get something to eat before your mother wakes up?"

180

What Kindness Is For

I came back to school three days after the fire, so sad that I felt almost numb. Even after Aunt Cat's pep talk, I felt like everything I had tried to do in my life was completely pointless. Every act of kindness and bravery had been a dead end. I couldn't protect anyone from anything, and every time I tried, it backfired. When I had tried to stand up for Nate, he had eventually decided to become pals with the kids who had picked on him. When I'd done it for Jamie, I had gotten my chest all ripped up and my dad's star broken.

Which I was pretty sure had not actually helped anybody.

And when I had finally gotten the guts to stand up for my mom against Johnny, she had thanked me by getting so drunk she had burned down our apartment and killed Freddy.

Some hero I was. I couldn't even help a freaking hamster.

It was time to give up, throw in the towel, and accept my destiny as a plain old shrimpy loser.

With those fun thoughts running again and again through my head, I trudged through the halls—which were empty, because of course I was late. My mom was ready to be released from the hospital, because she was almost completely recovered from the fire. She wasn't going to come right home, though, because after some long talks with Aunt Cat and a therapist, she had decided to go straight from the hospital to a two-month alcohol-rehabilitation treatment program. Aunt Cat had insisted we stop by the hospital to see my mother one more time before she went into rehab, so now I had one more tardy mark on my record, and the front of my shirt was damp with my mom's tears.

All I could think about was the last conversation I'd had with my mother. I had asked her why she had never told me what my father had really been like. She had replied, "I just wanted you to have a hero."

I'd told her, "Well, now's your chance to be my hero."

I had no idea whether she would come through. Of course I wanted her to, but I also didn't want to get my hopes up too high.

I walked into Mrs. Sakofsky's room, and everybody's heads whipped around to face me. It was a little bit freaky, and definitely not something I was in the mood for. Mrs. Sakofsky said, "Welcome back, Maverick! Your classmates have a little presentation for you."

Oh, perfect.

To my complete and utter horror, Nate and Bowen were the first two people to stand up, followed by several of their other MU friends. Two of the guys were carrying a huge rectangular box. With airholes in it.

Nate said, "We're, uh, all really sorry about what happened to your, um, house and everything. So a few of us were talking after soccer practice one day, and our field is right near the pet store, and we decided to see whether the whole class might want to chip in and get you a welcome-back present."

The two boys with the box started ripping it open. I was biting my lip as hard as I could, thinking, *But it's not the same. It's not the same it's not the same it's not the same . . .*

"We know it's not the same as having, um, Freddy back . . ." Nate said.

"But we thought it would be too disgusting to bite off one of his feet," Bowen continued, grinning.

I know it was horrible, but as most of the class gasped in horror, I actually let out a little half chuckle. Don't judge— it was funny.

Nate finished his original thought as though Bowen hadn't said anything. ". . . but we thought he might help make you feel better anyway. So, uh, yeah."

By then the box was one hundred percent unwrapped. It contained a huge glass terrarium, a new hanging water bottle, gigantic bags of food and wood shavings, an exercise wheel, several running tubes, and one chubby, nervous-looking hamster.

I felt my heart slamming away in my scarred chest. Everybody was looking right at me again, waiting for me to do something. Jamie must have seen something in my face, because she got up and stood next to me.

Then Bowen reached down into the enclosure and gently picked up the hamster. He said, "Come on, Falconer. The guy at the store says it doesn't bite."

Just then, the animal peed all over the sleeve of Bowen's jacket.

My heart settled down a bit. *All right*, I thought, reaching for the hamster. *I kind of like him.*

"What are you going to name him?" Jamie asked.

"Freddy Junior," I said.

But I should have said Frederica, because a week later, I came home to Aunt Cat's living room and found ten little baby hamsters clinging to her belly. Needless to say, this caused some panic, a quick trip to the pet store, and some negotiation with Bill. I walked out of there with a whole lot of instructions on the care and feeding of baby hamsters. It turned out I would have to keep the babies together and alive for six weeks, and then I would have to give them away to separate homes. I also got ten twenty-five-percent-off coupons for pet supplies. Aunt Cat walked out with a big smile on her face and a date for the following Friday night.

The next day in homeroom, I asked for volunteers to adopt the babies. Mrs. Sakofsky took one. So did Jamie. So did Nate and four other soccer players. Then Bowen came over to me, grabbed one of the twenty-five-percent-off coupons, and whispered, "Don't think this makes us, like, best pals or anything."

I whispered back, "Oh, please." But we both kind of smiled, just the tiniest little bit.

By the end of the day, the last two coupons had been taken, by Mr. Kurt and Mr. Overbye. Picturing the dreaded

Bee cuddling with a teeny-tiny baby rodent was a bit alarming. But then again, it kind of wasn't.

And at least The Bird hadn't tried to claim one.

Six weeks later, I met everybody at the pet store, where they all bought their supplies and took their babies.

It's weird. I used to get a little bit scared every time I saw a black jacket with gold lettering coming my way in the hall. Now I just think, *Hey, that guy chipped in to buy Frederica!*

Things change.

And maybe this whole thing has taught me something about what kindness is for. Because, looking back at this year, I still basically *did* fail when I tried to protect everybody. But that doesn't mean my efforts didn't matter. Maybe kindness spreads slowly, and even fails for a while, but then sort of seeps through again and keeps moving outward, until you suddenly find yourself surrounded by a ring of fellow hamster owners who used to be your enemies.

One More Little Meeting
with The Bee

Just when I thought everything had settled down, and I was getting used to my new life with Aunt Cat, The Bee called me down to his office. When I got there, he was smiling.

I didn't like that. It made me nervous. When I'm nervous, I sometimes talk too much.

"What?" I asked. "I haven't done anything. I've been getting good grades. Well, not super good, but better. And I've been on time every day for, like, a month. That's a record. You can look it up. I haven't gotten in any fights. I haven't even gotten in any almost-fights. The other day, I gave Bowen Strack half of my cookie at lunch. No, seriously. I did! Why are you laughing? Did you call me down here because we never talked about the whole Aunt-Cat-is-my-mother thing?

Because I can explain. It would feel great to get that all off my chest. I wasn't trying to make a fool out of you or anything. Not that I made a fool out of you. I mean, you're not a fool. You are a very smart-seeming guy. Man. Assistant principal person. Shutting up now."

"Are you sure you're finished?" The Bee asked.

I nodded.

"Good. You aren't in trouble, Maverick. I had a long talk with your aunt Catherine several weeks ago about your living situation. In fact, we have chatted weekly since your mother's accident. I've been quite concerned about you, but it seems like you're in capable hands. Your aunt is a remarkable woman. Are you happy in her home?"

I thought about that. Was I happy? Almost everything I owned had been destroyed in the fire. On the other hand, aside from Freddy, my star, and (once upon a time) my dad's medal, I had never really had any possessions that meant anything to me.

Who was I kidding? I had never really had any possessions, period.

And hey, at least Johnny's tree had gotten what it deserved.

Plus, I sort of had friends now. All the hamsters were thriving so far, and each person who'd taken one seemed to enjoy reporting to me on their new pet's progress several times a week. I was like the Hamster Godfather.

Life with Aunt Cat was stable. I had real food to eat. Her cooking was improving, too. When she made eggs and toast, it included eggs a lot of the time, and once there was even bacon. Or at least, the package *said* it was bacon. I also had brand-new clothing that I had actually gotten to pick out at real stores. Aunt Cat asked me about school every day, and remembered everything I told her. Sometimes Bill would bring takeout food over for dinner, and we would all play board games or watch a movie. I was learning for the first time that spending time with an adult couple didn't have to be scary. I wasn't completely ready to relax about it yet, and I wasn't sure Aunt Cat was either, but it was a start.

Still, my mother was basically locked up. If I said I was happy, did that make me a terrible person?

"I don't know. I love Aunt Cat, but I miss my mother." I wasn't even sure how true that was, but it felt like something I was supposed to say.

The Bee nodded, and then he said, "Maverick, I'm sure this is a crazy, upside-down time in your life, but I just want you to know my door is always open to you. All right?"

"Yes, Mr. Overbye."

"Now, there is one more thing. Class elections are coming up in a couple of months, and whoever wins the title of seventh-grade president for next fall will be working quite closely with me on items such as school rules, procedures for keeping the hallways running smoothly, and opening-day procedures. Somehow, when I thought of those topics, your name popped into my head immediately."

He paused, leaned back with his hands folded on his stomach, and looked at me.

"Umm, sir, are you asking *me* to run for class president?"

"Yes, I am. Or at least, I'm asking you to consider it."

"Why? I get in trouble all the time. My life is a mess. There are a million kids around here who are more popular than I am, and smarter, and better behaved."

"I think you would be a great class president because you have leadership qualities. Granted, they're in a somewhat rough form right now, but I think you could be a great president. Think about it: Whenever you see something you don't think is right, what do you do?"

"I charge in there, bang the wrong kid into a locker door, and get sent to the office. Or I charge in there, get strangled from behind by a girl, and then get sent to the office. Or I charge in there, get sliced open, and get sent to the hospital. I think those are the basic options."

The Bee leaned forward, grinned, and pounded his fist on the desk. "Right! That's what makes you different! You charge in there!"

"What about all the other stuff? You know, the fights? The getting in trouble? The bleeding?"

"We can work on all that. In fact, I think you already have been working on that. Think about it—how many enemies have you turned into friends this year?"

I thought about it. "I don't know. A few, I guess."

"*More* than a few, *I* guess. Anyway, listen. You stand up to people, even people who have power over you. I don't think you have any idea how rare that is. Think about the people you know. What do they do when they are face-to-face with a bully? When they see someone being picked on? When they see a chance to right a wrong? And how many of them have as much success as you do? Don't answer me for a little while . . . just think about it."

I thought about it. I didn't really know anybody else who tried to stop people from being bullied, but I certainly knew a whole lot of people who had been pushed around. Some people who have been beaten or abused, like my mother, spend the rest of their lives trying to be nice to every bully they meet, thinking the next one won't turn and start swinging at them. But bullies are made for swinging. That's what they do.

Others, like Bowen, are so sure the world is full of nothing but bullies that they become bullies themselves, trying to hit everyone in the world first. But a life of getting in the first shot isn't a life. Not really, anyway.

Then there are people like my dad, who apparently handle their fear by charging face-first into every wall, who need to be the first man in and the last man out at every fire. Until the one time they don't make it out of the fire at all.

I wasn't sure what my path would be, but I knew I didn't want to be like any of them. Each, in their own way, spent life being ruled by the exact same things they feared.

Maybe the real heroes were people like Aunt Cat and—even though I couldn't believe I was thinking this—The Bee. They were the only ones I knew who reached down and helped the people coming up behind them to stand up. Maybe I could learn to be a leader if I just paid attention to how they did it.

Maybe I didn't need webs to be a hero—or rippling muscles, or a bulletproof shield. Maybe, at the end of the day, I could just keep trying to look around for people who needed a hand, and then grab on to theirs with my own.

But still, it would be nice if I could break the five-foot barrier someday. I'm just sayin'.

"All right, I'll do it. I have to warn you, though. I'll probably lose the election."

The Bee smiled.

"You know," I said, "I was really scared of you back in September. But you're not really scary at all."

He smiled even bigger. "Mr. Falconer, if you repeat what you just said to anyone outside this office, terrible . . . things . . . will . . . happen . . . to . . . you. **Understood?**"

I smiled back. "Uh-huh. Sure!"

On the way back to class, I thought about what had just happened. I figured I was right that I would probably lose the election, but I also realized I didn't need to be class president to continue my mission. It wasn't like Captain America was an elected position. Or Spider-Man. So why should the Secret Sheriff of Sixth Grade be any different?

But then I realized a name change was in order. I reached into my left front pocket, squeezed my trusty, glued-together badge, and squared my puny shoulders. I was still the smallest kid I knew. My home life was still up in the air, and it might always be. I was still afraid of many, many things. I still didn't know what I was doing half the time.

But soon enough, I would either be class president or the Secret Sheriff of Seventh Grade.

Sounded kind of epic to me.

About the Author

Jordan Sonnenblick is the author of many acclaimed novels, including *Drums, Girls & Dangerous Pie, Notes from the Midnight Driver, Zen and the Art of Faking It, Curveball: The Year I Lost My Grip, After Ever After*, and *Falling Over Sideways*. He lives in Bethlehem, Pennsylvania, with his family and numerous musical instruments. You can find out a whole lot more about him at jordansonnenblick.com.